"I need to get to work."

"Not on your own," Reuben stated.

"What do you propose I do? Run to the hired-hand store?" Leanne asked.

For the past three years, she had heard nothing from Reuben. A man she had given her heart to and so much more.

And now he'd swooped back into her life and told her what she should and shouldn't do on a ranch he'd walked away from? A ranch he'd never showed any interest in?

"I could help out until you're done," he said.

Her head spun and all she could do was stare at him. Reuben? Working alongside her on the ranch?

She shook her head. "No. That's not happening. We'll manage on our own."

"You won't and you know it," he returned.

She fought a confusing mix of anger and loss as she held his dark brown eyes. Eyes she was once lost in.

Focus. He's not the man you thought he was.

Carolyne Aarsen and her husband, Richard, live on a small ranch in northern Alberta, where they have raised four children and numerous foster children and are still raising cattle. Carolyne crafts her stories in an office with a large west-facing window, through which she can watch the changing seasons while struggling to make her words obey. Visit her website at carolyneaarsen.com.

Books by Carolyne Aarsen

Love Inspired

Cowboys of Cedar Ridge

Courting the Cowboy
Second-Chance Cowboy
The Cowboy's Family Christmas

Big Sky Cowboys

Wrangling the Cowboy's Heart
Trusting the Cowboy
The Cowboy's Christmas Baby

Lone Star Cowboy League

A Family for the Soldier

Refuge Ranch

Her Cowboy Hero
Reunited with the Cowboy
The Cowboy's Homecoming

Hearts of Hartley Creek

A Father's Promise
Unexpected Father
A Father in the Making

Visit the Author Profile page at Harlequin.com for more titles.

The Cowboy's Family Christmas

Carolyne Aarsen

Recycling programs for this product may not exist in your area.

LOVE INSPIRED BOOKS

ISBN-13: 978-0-373-89965-4

The Cowboy's Family Christmas

This edition published by arrangement with Love Inspired Books.

www.Harlequin.com

Printed in U.S.A.

You intended to harm me,
but God intended it for good.
—*Genesis* 50:20

For my grandkids. You've taught me
a whole new huge kind of love.

Chapter One

It was a surprisingly balmy Tuesday for November. Fall seemed reluctant to leave and Leanne Walsh was fine with that. She had too much to do on the ranch.

Late afternoon sunshine softened the day, creating gentle shadows on the Porcupine Hills of Alberta. A chill cooled the air, a threat of winter coming. Leanne hoped it hung off for at least a week. They still had cows to move down from the upper pastures and then had to process them.

Her son, Austin, sat astride the palomino mare his grandfather purchased a half a year ago when Austin was only two. Leanne had protested the expense but George Walsh insisted that Walshes learned to ride a proper horse as young as possible.

Now Austin was laughing down at her,

his shock of brown hair falling over his forehead, his chubby hands clutching the saddle horn, the cowboy hat he'd gotten a couple of weeks ago clamped firmly on his head. Since George had given it to Austin, he'd worn it nonstop.

"He looks comfortable up there." George stood by the fence, his arms hooked over the top rail, his battered cowboy hat pushed back on his head. Though he was only fifty-eight, Leanne's father-in-law looked twenty years older.

Life had knocked a lot out of the man, Leanne thought, acknowledging his gruff comment with a tight nod. He'd lost his first wife to cancer and was left with a young son, then he was abandoned by the second wife, leaving him with another young son. Dirk, his eldest son and Leanne's late husband, now lay buried in the graveyard abutting the church in Cedar Ridge, and the son of his second marriage, Reuben was so far out of George's life, he may as well be dead.

"Is that mare favoring her one leg?" George asked, concern edging his voice.

Leanne watched more carefully as the horse walked, each footfall of Heart's Delight's hooves raising small puffs of dust in the round pen. "I can't see it," she said glancing up at her son again, the sight of him pulling her mouth into a full smile. "But I'll keep an eye out."

"Not always easy for someone like you to catch that kind of thing."

Someone like you.

Though Leanne knew he spoke of her ability to read horses, those three simple words had the power to make her shoulders hunch and her hands clench the halter rope.

Those three words held a weight of history behind them. George had tossed them at her when he discovered that she, a Rennie, daughter of one of the most hated and useless men in Cedar Ridge, dared to think she could date his favored son, Dirk Walsh, let alone marry him.

"I know enough about horses to see if one is lame or not," she finally returned. "And if you have any further concerns, we can bring it to see Tabitha or Morgan." Her sister held an equine specialist degree and her fiancé, Morgan Walsh, was a vet. Together they were starting a new vet clinic on some acreage Tabitha owned close to town.

"Morgan doesn't even have his clinic done yet," George groused.

"It will be. But for now they can still diagnose any problems Heart's Delight might have."

George's only reply was a slight curl of his lip and she fought the urge to defend her sister. Leanne knew it was only because of her marriage to Dirk and because of his grandson, Austin, that George tolerated her presence.

Which had made her even more determined to prove herself to him. Prove she was worthy. As a result she spent every available minute working on the ranch. Showing that she could ride and rope better than any hired hand they had, including their latest, Chad. She did the bookkeeping and dealt with the accountant.

"Is Chad coming again tomorrow?" Leanne asked.

Their new hired hand had started a couple of days ago but hadn't come to work yesterday and called in sick today. Which made her wonder if she would have to start looking for another hired hand all over again.

"He said he would. Though I don't know why you hired him. He doesn't know much about cows or horses," George grumbled.

"He's willing and I think he can be trained." She wanted to say more but the sound of a truck engine caught both their attentions.

The ranch was nestled in a valley, well off the main road snaking through the hills. People arriving at the ranch had to drive along a switchback road that traversed the hill leading down to the ranch. If they didn't know the road, it could be trouble. And this person was driving far too fast.

"Idiot is going to overshoot the second turn," George muttered, pushing away from the fence, irritation edging his voice. "Probably some salesman who doesn't know how to drive his fancy truck in the back of the beyond."

But whoever it was seemed to know the road because, in spite of the speed of the vehicle, the truck easily made it around the corner and then down the tree-lined road toward the ranch. It suddenly slowed at the cattle guard, and as it rattled across, unease niggled through Leanne.

Though the driver seemed familiar with the approach to the Bar W Ranch, Leanne didn't recognize the black truck with the gleaming grill getting coated with dust.

It made the tight bend past the house, then came toward the corrals. As the driver killed the engine, silence fell again.

The door opened and a tall, broad-shouldered man stepped out wearing a cowboy hat over his collar-length hair. Sunglasses shaded his face and he dropped a cell phone into the pocket of a worn twill shirt, the sleeves rolled up over muscular forearms. Faded blue jeans hugged his hips and his boots were scuffed and worn at the heel.

He started walking toward them with the easy rolling gait of a man who had spent time on a horse. Definitely not a salesman.

"Can I help you?" George asked, the irritation in his voice shifting to aggression.

Leanne groaned. *Please, Lord*, she prayed as she led Austin and his horse to the rail fence, *don't let this be one of the officials from the association who promised to come and visit someday.*

Seeing George in full-on Walsh mode wouldn't help their cause. She was the temporary secretary for the Cedar Ridge Rodeo Group. For the past couple years the group had tried to get their town's rodeo to be a part of the larger Milk River Rodeo Association. They needed all the goodwill they could muster.

"This is private land," George continued as the man drew closer.

"Here, punkin, why don't you come down?" Leanne asked, tying up the horse and reaching for Austin. She had to intervene before George took a notion to grab the shotgun stashed in the barn behind them.

Leanne lifted her son over the fence, clambered over herself, picked Austin up, then hurried over to where her father-in-law stood, hands planted on his hips, head thrust forward in an aggressive gesture. "What's your business here?" George growled.

But the stranger was unfazed by George's belligerence. A slow smile crawled across his well-shaped mouth, shaded by a scruff of whiskers, and the unease in Leanne grew.

"Hey, George," the man said, sweeping his sunglasses off, tucking them in the pocket of his shirt and flicking his cowboy hat back. "Been a few years."

Leanne's legs suddenly went numb. Her heart turned to ice at the sound of that voice. At the sight of those brown eyes, crinkled at the corners.

Reuben Walsh.

Prodigal son come home.

And right behind all her initial reactions came a wave of anger so fierce it threatened to swamp her.

Reuben Walsh had known his father wouldn't throw out the welcome mat when he saw him nor kill the fatted calf when he arrived. And he had guessed Leanne wouldn't be thrilled either.

But the blatant rage in her narrowed eyes was unexpected.

The last time he'd seen her, she'd been lying in a hospital bed, her auburn hair tied up in a tangled ponytail he knew would have driven her crazy. Leanne always wore her thick hair loose, hanging halfway down her back. Always had her nails perfectly done. Always looked amazing even in the simple clothes she tended to wear.

But at that time she lay unconscious, her pale features slack as if she were as dead as her husband, Dirk, was. His brother, Dirk.

She and Dirk had been on their way back from their honeymoon after a quick and unexpected wedding that happened before Reuben had flown back to Cedar Ridge.

To propose to Leanne himself.

He stopped in at the hospital to see her after his brother's funeral, stood by her bed, the angry questions swirling around his mind unable to be asked, and then he left. Taking his ring and his broken heart with him. He hadn't been back since. Nor had he and Leanne been in contact.

What could they possibly have to say to each other?

"Hey, Leanne," he said, surprised at the hitch in his voice when their eyes met.

To his surprise and disappointment, old feelings gripped his heart.

For years she had occupied his waking thoughts and drifted through his dreams. Now here she stood, Dirk's widow, with his nephew resting on her hip. Two reminders of the distance between them.

"Hey, Reuben."

Her voice was cool and clipped. He felt his own ire rise up, wondering what right she had to be bent out of shape.

"What are you doing here?" His father's gruff voice grated and once again Reuben fought the old inferiority his father always created in him.

When Reuben received the email from Owen Herne, chairman of the Cedar Ridge Rodeo Group, asking him to assess the unfinished arena for them, he'd been tempted to delete it. He had no desire to return to Cedar Ridge and face the woman he had loved, now the widow of his forever-favored older brother. And why would he deliberately put himself in the line of his father's constant disapproval? He had lived with that long enough when he was a teenager.

The last time he was in Cedar Ridge was three years ago to attend his brother's funeral. George had been so bitter, he hadn't acknowledged Reuben's presence. No personal greeting. No question about how he was doing. No recognition of Reuben's own pain at the loss of a brother.

As for Leanne, she'd still been unconscious and in the hospital. While seeing her so incapacitated had gutted him, in some twisted way it was probably for the best. Reuben wouldn't have known what to say to her after she'd left him for his brother.

But the tiny part of him that still clung to hope pushed him to come home.

"Owen asked me to come talk to the Rodeo Group. About the arena," Reuben said, determined not to let these two show how much influence they had over his life and emotions.

"He never said anything to me," George complained.

"You'll have to take that up with him," Reuben said, trying to keep his tone light and conversational. "But the ranch was on my way to town. I thought I would stop by and say hello."

"It's been a long time since you were here," George said.

On this point Reuben couldn't fault him, though he stifled a beat of resentment at his father's frowning disapproval. Didn't matter what he did when he was growing up, George criticized him.

Come home with good marks?

Well, he could have done better.

Ride the rankest bronc in the rodeo?

Could have scored higher.

Never as good as his brother. Never as good as Dirk.

"It has been awhile," Reuben agreed. He wasn't apologizing for his lack. As the son of the wife who had taken off, Reuben often felt his father held him to account for his mother's behavior. And Reuben had taken that on, as well, always trying to find ways to earn his gruff father's approval.

But it never happened. In fact George had made it clear Dirk would take over the ranch when he was old enough and that there was no place for Reuben in spite of all the work he had done here year after year. Reuben left home as soon as he graduated high school. He rode rodeo in the summer and took on any odd job to help pay for his structural engineering classes. He was determined to show his father he could go it alone. Now he had a degree and had already racked up some impressive jobs. Though his heart had always been here in Cedar Ridge, once he discovered that Dirk and Leanne had had a baby, he shelved any hope of coming back.

His eyes drifted again to Leanne, the

woman who, at one time, he had dared to weave dreams and plans around.

"So, here we are," he said.

Instead of responding, she set his nephew, Austin, on his feet and clung to his chubby little hand. She adjusted the little cowboy hat he wore, then glanced over at George.

Looking everywhere but at him as a tense silence fell between them.

Since she'd moved here with her sister, Tabitha, and her father when she was in high school, Leanne Rennie had only had eyes for his older brother, Dirk. And he knew why. Dirk was the good brother. Steady. Solid. Dependable. A Christian.

Reuben knew exactly who he was. The irresponsible younger brother who could only worship Leanne from afar.

Though Leanne had dated his brother for years and been engaged to Dirk for four of them, Reuben had never been able to completely let go of his feelings for her.

But Dirk held off on setting a wedding date for four years. Then, as if she couldn't wait any longer, Leanne broke up with Dirk. His brother left for Europe, and he and Leanne met up at his cousin's destination wedding in Costa Rica. They'd spent two glorious weeks together. She'd confessed that, while she had always wanted the security Dirk could offer, she had a hard time denying her changing feelings for Reuben.

They decided they wanted to be together but she had said that she needed to tell Dirk first. Reuben couldn't figure out why, but he gave Leanne the space she asked for.

Then when Dirk came back from his trip, the next thing he heard, via his cousin Cord, was that Dirk and Leanne had eloped. Reuben was devastated, hurt, then the anger kicked in and he threw himself into his work. He was determined to prove he didn't need anyone. That he could be successful.

And he had accomplished that. In two weeks he would be starting with a company that promised him prestige and financial independence.

He thought he had put Leanne out of his mind for good, but seeing her now, even more beautiful than he remembered, created an unwelcome hitch in his heart.

In the uncomfortable silence that lingered, a bird warbled, and the wind rustled through the trees sheltering the house beyond them. No one said anything more.

"Well, just thought I'd stop by and say hi." He looked away from his father and Leanne, then crouched down in front of Austin. "And

I thought I would get to know you, little guy. I'm your uncle Reuben."

Austin pursed his lips, frowning slightly, as if he didn't believe he had an uncle.

The idea that his only nephew didn't even know who he was cut almost as deep as Leanne's chilly attitude.

"Wooben," Austin said finally. "Uncle Wooben."

"That's right."

Austin stared at him then pointed at Reuben's hat, then his own, looking proud. "My hat. I have my hat."

"It's a pretty cool hat," Reuben agreed.

But then Austin looked up at Leanne, no longer interested in his uncle. "Firsty, Mommy."

"We'll get something in a minute, sweetheart." Leanne hesitated, then glanced over at Reuben, her eyes barely skimming over him. "Would you like some tea?"

"He might not have time," his father said, as if Reuben was no more than a salesman whom George felt he had to be polite to.

Reuben pushed himself up, glancing from his father back to Leanne. He guessed her invitation was more a formality than anything. That his father could be so cool to him he fully understood. Nothing new there.

But Leanne? The woman he had, at one time, thought would be his?

"No. I should get going," Reuben said, fighting down his own resentment and anger.

Good thing the opinion of other people had never mattered to him. Otherwise this could have been a genuinely painful moment.

"Will you be coming by again?" his father asked.

"I'll have to see how things go" was all he would say. No sense in pushing himself on either his father or his sister-in-law if he didn't have to.

George turned to Leanne. "I'm going back to the house."

Then without another word to Reuben, he walked away, shoulders bent, head down.

He looked much older than the last time Reuben had seen him, and in spite of his father's lack of welcome and veiled animosity, Reuben felt the sting of remorse that he'd stayed away so long.

It wasn't your fault.

Maybe not, but he should have been the bigger man. Should have set aside the old hurts and slights. In spite of how George treated him, he was still Reuben's father.

He set aside his regrets for now and looked to Leanne, guessing he would get neither handshake nor hug from her. Not the way she stared daggers at him. As if she had any right.

"So we might see you around?" she asked. The chill in her voice almost made him shudder.

But then, to his surprise, she held his gaze a beat longer than necessary and once again the old feelings came back.

"I'm sure. It's a small town," he returned, then he turned to Austin and gave the little boy a quick grin. "So, I'll see you again," he said to his nephew.

"Bring a present?" Austin asked.

"Austin, that's not polite." Leanne gave her son's hand a gentle reprimanding shake.

"I should have thought of that," Reuben said with a light laugh. "After all, I am your uncle and uncles should come with presents."

"I like horses. My dad liked horses."

Reuben's heart twisted. Once again his and Leanne's eyes met.

"I never had a chance to tell you how sorry I was to hear about Dirk," he said, thumbing his hat back. As if to see her better.

"He was your brother too." Leanne's voice held a thread of sorrow and for a moment they acknowledged their shared grief.

"He was a good brother. And I'm sure he was a good husband."

Leanne released a harsh laugh. "I hardly had the chance to find out. We were only married two weeks." She pressed her lips together and Reuben took a quick step toward her. Before he even knew what he was doing he laid a gentle hand on her shoulder, tightening it enough to let her know that he understood.

She stayed where she was a moment, but then jerked back, her features growing hard. She turned to Austin. "I'll get you a drink, sweetie, but first we should put your horse away."

Then she left, Austin trailing alongside her, her head held high, back stiff, exuding waves of rejection.

"Bye, Uncle Wooben," Austin called out, looking back.

Reuben waved goodbye. It was time for him to leave but he waited, watching Leanne as she walked down the grassy path toward the corrals where a horse stood, waiting patiently. She told Austin to stay where he was as she climbed over the fence.

He wanted to ask her why she thought she had the right to be so angry with him when she was the one who'd run back to his brother as soon as Dirk came back into her life. Ask her what happened to those promises they made to each other in Costa Rica. When she had told him that she'd always cared for him.

Had they all been lies?

He spun around, striding back to his truck. That duty was done. He wished he had listened to the realistic part of himself and simply driven past this place and the two people who didn't want him around.

Reuben slipped his sunglasses on and climbed into his truck. He started it up and, without a backward glance, drove off the ranch that had been his home for years.

He and Leanne were over. He had to look to his own future.

And as he drove, he second-guessed his plan to work in Cedar Ridge for the Rodeo Group.

He glanced back at the ranch as it grew smaller in his rearview mirror.

Why should he put himself through this on purpose?

He would talk to Owen Herne. Tell him he wasn't taking on the job. He had no reason at all to stay in town.

Tomorrow he'd leave and Cedar Ridge would only be a memory.

Chapter Two

"I know I put you on the spot, but I don't have much choice." Reuben rolled his coffee cup back and forth between his hands, looking everywhere but at his cousin Cord and his Uncle Boyce sitting across from him at the Brand and Grill. "I can't do this job."

The muted hum of conversation and the occasional order called out by Adana, one of the waitresses, filled the silence that followed his pronouncement.

Cord Walsh lifted one hand, his green-grey eyes narrowed. "You said you were willing," he said. "We could have gotten someone else, but you said you could do this. We don't have much time to get this done."

"I know that, but I also know what I can and can't do."

"Did your other job get moved up?" Boyce

asked, swiping his plate with the last bite of toast. "That why you changed your mind?"

"No. It still doesn't start for a couple of weeks but…" He hesitated, wondering what to say without sounding like some heartsick loser. "I don't think coming back was a good idea." He pushed his coffee cup away from him and sat back, as well. He didn't want to say any more than that in front of his uncle, George's brother.

Boyce was busy taking one last swig of his coffee. But Cord held his gaze for an extra beat as if delving into Reuben's thoughts.

If anyone knew Reuben's history, it was his cousin. Cord knew most of Reuben's secrets. Most, not all. The only other cousin who understood where Reuben was coming from was Noah. He also had to deal with a father who was never satisfied.

"Okay, then," Cord said with an air of resignation, glancing at his father. "I'm guessing we can't change your mind with our Walsh charm or appeal to your Walsh heritage."

Reuben chuckled. "Probably not. I'm immune to those tactics." Then he reached into the pocket of his denim jacket and pulled out a folded piece of paper. He pushed it across the table to Cord. "Here are the names of a couple of other guys you could get. They haven't made any firm commitments and they won't be available for a month or so. But they're good too." After his disastrous visit to his father's ranch, Reuben had made a few calls from the motel to some other engineers he knew. He got a couple of vague commitments from some old classmates. It was the best he could do under the circumstances.

"So tell us about this job you're starting," Boyce said, looking up as Cord pocketed the note. Clearly his uncle wasn't going to try to convince Reuben to stay. "I haven't heard anything about it from George."

Reuben wasn't surprised. He knew George didn't talk often about him. "It's a good position with a prestigious international engineering firm. I'd be my own boss, which is what I've been looking for since I graduated," Reuben said, thankful for his uncle's switch in topic. He didn't want to expound on the real reasons he was leaving. Leanne and Austin, the visible reminder of her betrayal of Reuben. "I'll be making good money and I'll be traveling around the world doing some big jobs. What's not to like?"

"And there's no one in your life right now who would object to all the moving around?" Boyce asked.

Reuben shook his head. "Nope. Haven't met anyone who created any sparks."

"I get where you're coming from," Cord said. "I think Ella and I had sparks the first time we met."

"Didn't help that Adana had just quit as your nanny and you were ticked off," Boyce said with a laugh.

"There was more than that going on." Cord grinned and then his phone dinged. He glanced at it, then back at Reuben. "I gotta deal with this. Are you leaving today?"

Reuben nodded. The sooner the better.

"Then I'll say goodbye."

"I'm heading out too," Boyce said, "Though I wouldn't mind sticking around and talking more, I sense you want to get a move on." He gave Reuben a rueful smile, which, more than anything either of them had said, made Reuben second-guess his decision.

But then he thought of Leanne's anger and his father's lack of affection, and he knew he wasn't ready to put himself in that vulnerable position.

"Much as I'd like to connect with some of the other cousins, I feel I should get going."

Cord got up the same time Reuben did and pulled him close in a quick, man hug then stepped back, holding his gaze. "You stay safe and don't be a stranger."

"I won't," he said.

Then Boyce dropped some bills on the table to pay for breakfast, got up and gave him a tighter hug than Cord had. "I've been praying for you," he said as he pulled back. "You and your father."

Reuben felt a twinge of guilt at the sentiment. After Dirk's funeral and Leanne's betrayal, he had kept his distance from God. Only in the past few months had he realized how much he missed his faith and started attending church again.

"Thanks. I probably need it," he said, keeping his tone light.

"You'll be back for my wedding, won't you?" Cord asked as they made their way out of the restaurant.

"I hope so. I'll have to see what my new work schedule is. I'll be needing to impress some big investors."

"This job sounds serious," Boyce said as he slowly made his way down the few steps out of the café. "And important."

"I've got a lot riding on it and the pay is amazing." This job was his chance to prove to himself that he had value. Worth.

"Well, you know, it's a cliché but money isn't everything," Boyce said.

"No, but it's a fairly universal measuring stick. One that your brother, George, understands."

Cord gave him a curious look but Reuben wasn't delving deeper into the past. He had a promising future ahead of him and in spite of feeling bad that he had let his cousin and his uncle down, he had to move on. Staying in Cedar Ridge wasn't an option.

"Well, you take care. Stay in touch and don't be such a stranger."

Reuben nodded as he buttoned his denim jacket closed. The wind still held a chill. It was cooler than yesterday and as he walked down the street to his truck, he shivered as he thought of California, where he would be headquartered.

It would be warm there. No snow and no winter. Just sun and warmth and work.

Boyce and Cord said goodbye and left.

Reuben watched them leave and felt a twinge of melancholy when they both laughed at something Cord had said. How often had he longed for a relationship like his cousin and uncle shared?

He shook off the feelings, walked to his

truck, drove down Main Street, then headed to the highway out of town.

But as he drove away from Cedar Ridge, he tried not to think that he might not be back for a very, very long time.

His father's ranch was on his way out of town, and as he came nearer he was tempted to keep going. Drive on into his future and leave the past behind. But he knew guilt and second thoughts would follow him all the way back to Calgary, so he slowed as he came to the wooden and stone archway leading to the ranch. Hanging from the cross bar was the ranch's brand, stamped on a metal disc. The Bar W. And with it hung the weight of the Walsh legacy and their prominence in the community of Cedar Ridge.

This was driven home when he drove up to the imposing bulk of the ranch house once again. It was built to impress and easily fulfilled that promise. The house spread out and upward, two stories high. The main part of the house, directly in front of him, held the main living area. Kitchen, great room, family room, formal dining room, kitchen nook. Two wings stretched out from the main house. One wing held the master bedroom, a media room, an office and a guest bedroom. The other was where Reuben and Dirk had slept and also had an extra bedroom.

Reuben's mother had often said that the family rattled around in the large space. She was right, but the space also gave Reuben places to retreat to after his mother left. Away from George's steady criticism.

Reuben parked on the cement pad in front of the large, four-bay garage, guessing that Leanne and George's vehicles were inside.

He stayed in the truck a moment, taking a breath, readying himself to face them again. At least this time he was prepared.

He got out of the truck and strode to the house. But when he rang the doorbell no one answered. He put his head inside and called out, but again, only silence.

Puzzled he walked past the house and the gardens Dirk's mother had started, surprised to see them all cleaned up and obviously cared for. His mother had never cared for them and they had been taken over by weeds and neglect.

Leanne must have revived the garden. He remembered how she had often wished she could fix it up when she and Dirk were dating.

He stopped again, listening for voices. Maybe they were all gone. He went a little farther and as he came over the rise separating the ranch house from the corrals, he heard the distinctive lowing of cattle and the bawl of baby calves.

He walked around the grove of trees between the garden behind the house and the cow corrals lying in a hollow tucked against the hill the house stood on.

The sound of shouting and the bellowing of cows grew louder as he got closer. Some cows stood in the pasture along the rugged fence, bawling for their calves, which had been separated from them in another large pen.

The rest of the cows were on the other side, milling about, creating a cloud of dust as they waited to be processed.

That's when he saw her. Leanne was mounted on a large palomino, wearing a down vest, her hair tied back. Her hat was shoved on her head and she waved a coil of rope as she pushed the horse into a crush of bawling animals, cutting some away.

What was she doing? That was dangerous work. She could be hurt. There were far too many cows in the pen. Why was she working with them?

An unfamiliar man stood by a gate connected to another smaller pen. Clearly his job was to open the gate when enough cows were cut out of the herd. A younger man sat astride a horse, a ball cap clamped over his dark hair.

"Devin, get over there," he heard his father yelling. Big surprise. Dad's default emotion was anger. "Stop being so ridiculously lazy and help out," he bellowed again from his position on the raised walkway by the fenced-in alley adjacent the pen.

He sounded so angry. If George wasn't careful, he would have a heart attack someday. Reuben hurried his pace to see if he could help out. Leanne shouldn't be doing what she was.

She was on one edge of the milling cattle, keeping them moving; Devin was working his way through the herd.

But when George yelled again, the young man pulled his horse to a stop, leaning on his saddle horn as if making a decision.

"Get in there," his father shouted, looking ready to climb over the fence and help out himself. "Get those cows moving."

The young man named Devin kept his horse where it was, then finally he made a move.

Only it wasn't into the cattle to help Leanne cut some out. It was in the other direction. Away from the cows.

Toward the gate leading out of the pen.

As he came closer, Reuben easily saw the angry set of the young man's jaw, the determined way he urged his horse toward the large metal gate separating the cows from one of the pastures. He dismounted and unlatched the gate, ignoring Leanne's cries and George's fury. His movements were rushed and jerky, the chain clanking against the gate. It was as if he couldn't contain himself any longer.

He had Reuben's complete sympathy. Reuben knew what it was like to be on the receiving end of George's demands. Never feeling like the job you were doing was good enough. Always getting pushed to do more. He wondered how long this young man had worked for his father.

"Devin. Where are you going?" Leanne called out, the concern in her voice evident from here.

"Get back here, Devin," George yelled. "Get back here or you're fired."

"You can't fire me," Devin shouted back, his voice filled with rage as he shoved open the gate, "because I quit."

Then Devin led his horse through the open gate.

But he hadn't looked behind him. Reuben could easily see what the young man, in his fury, had missed.

A group of cows and calves had followed Devin and his horse and were right behind him as he turned to close the gate.

Too late he noticed the animals and struggled to shut the gate on them. But by then the cows were already pushing past him to freedom. Devin jumped back, pulling his horse back, the cows now streaming out of the gate.

From what Reuben remembered, if the cows got away, they would run toward the open fields behind the ranch and from there up into the foothill pastures, which were spread out over hundreds and hundreds of acres. If they got too far out, it would take days to round them up again. Maybe even longer once the cows had gotten their taste of freedom.

"Devin, close that gate," George yelled, leaning over the fence, his face purple. "Close the gate, you useless twerp."

But Devin had given up and was leading his horse away from the herd flowing through the gate.

Reuben grabbed hold of a fence post and clambered over in his hurry to catch the gate and stop the rest of the cows from getting out. But it was hard to halt the press of all those large bodies and too dangerous.

"What did you do?" he called out to Devin, who was ignoring the herd racing past him as he walked along the fence.

"I quit." Devin muttered as Reuben tried to get by him. "George is a maniac boss."

"Is that your own horse?" Reuben asked as the cows, increasing in number, now thundered past them.

"No. Belongs to the ranch."

That's all he needed to know. Reuben yanked the reins out of Devin's hand, did a quick assessment of the young man's height. They were about the same. The stirrups should be okay.

Then he vaulted into the saddle, turned the horse around, nudged him in the flanks and galloped off to head off the cows before they got too far away.

It was a race and Reuben had to be careful not to get too close to the cows and get them running even faster. He heard Leanne's shout and tossed a quick glance over his shoulder to see her following on horseback behind him, making a wide loop around the herd like he had.

All he could hear now was the thundering of the cows' hooves, the steady rhythm of the horse's, its hard breathing and Leanne shouting something indecipherable.

* * *

She needed to catch up to Reuben. Leanne gripped the reins of her horse, urging it on, fighting to stay in the saddle of the racing horse.

She shoved down a beat of panic as she galloped alongside the now running herd going faster than she thought possible.

She didn't have time to plan. All she could concentrate on was getting the herd turned around before they got too far ahead. Could they do it with two horses? She'd never handled a charging herd before.

Please, Lord, help me keep my seat. Help me not fall off.

Her prayer was automatic. She didn't want to disgrace herself in front of either Reuben, who seemed to be one with the horse he rode, or George, who had seemed on the verge of having a heart attack when the cows had surged through the open gate.

She was so angry with Devin, but right now she couldn't spare him much thought.

Slowly the gap between their horses lessened and, to her surprise and relief, Reuben managed to get his horse in front of the lead cows. He waved his hat at the herd as he pulled his horse's speed in.

Please don't split, she silently pleaded as

she came behind Reuben, trying to gauge the correct distance between her and Reuben and the cows. Too close and she would spook the herd. Too far back and some of the cows might go right between them and they'd have two bunches to worry about.

Thankfully they stayed together, calves bawling, cows bellowing and dust rising up from the milling hooves.

Reuben made it to the front of the herd and slowly, slowly their forward momentum decreased. Reuben waved his hat again, yelling to get the cows turned. But the animals behind didn't know what was happening and kept running through, ramming into the cows in the front. This spooked them again and Leanne hurried to join Reuben at the front to hold the herd back.

But finally the animals seemed to sense they weren't going to carry on and the herd slowed its pace, Reuben and Leanne keeping up.

"Don't get too close," Reuben called out. "Stay far enough away that they can see you but not get scared again."

Leanne nodded, pulling her horse back.

Reuben waved his arm at the cows again and they stopped. "Get beside me but stay about ten feet away," he shouted to Leanne.

"Turn your horse toward the cows and keep it facing them."

Leanne simply did what she was told. Reuben had herded far more cows than she had and knew what he was doing.

So she turned her horse around, her heart pounding in her chest with a mixture of fear and anticipation as she faced down the herd in front of her. The cows had their heads up as if looking for a way out. What would happen now depended on the decision of the lead cows.

"Get along, you creatures," Reuben yelled, waving his hat at them again. Leanne had left her rope behind and her hat had tumbled off somewhere in the pasture so she waved her hands, praying it would help.

Then, together, they managed to get the front cows turned back toward the corrals and, thankfully, the others reluctantly followed suit.

The herd pushed and bawled as they made their way back, expressing their disappointment and confusion.

"You keep pressure on the herd, I'll make sure they stay bunched," Reuben called out.

Again all Leanne could do was nod.

A few calves made a break from the herd, heading for the upper pastures but Reuben quickly got them back, his horse easily stopping and turning them around.

Thankfully his horse was a seasoned cutting horse and Reuben knew what he was doing.

The cattle had their heads down now, plodding along the way cows should be moving. Leanne sneezed on the dust raised by the herd walking over the fields that were once green. She shivered as the worst of the drama was over.

Reuben was still working the one side of the herd as the animals headed back to the corrals. She knew they would face another challenge when they came to the gate, but hopefully the bale of hay she'd put inside the pen to lure them in the first place would draw them back again. The pasture they were riding on now was brown and chewed down so there was nothing to entice them here, though a few cows slowed to check it out.

As they got closer to the yard, she saw the gate was still open. George was on the other side of the fence, holding it with a rope to make sure it didn't swing shut. He also knew what to do.

Then, finally, the first cows went through the gate.

"Push them harder," Reuben called out,

whistling at the cows. "We need to get them moving fast enough so the front ones get pushed farther into the corrals and don't decide to turn around when they reach the end."

Leanne clucked to her horse, urging the cows on, and then, finally, they were all back in the corrals and the large metal gate clanged shut behind them.

Her hands were shaking as she unclenched the reins and pulled in a long, steadying breath. They had come so close to a complete disaster.

If Reuben hadn't been there right when Devin quit…

She shut that thought off. She didn't know why Reuben had returned, but he had, and right now she was relieved to have the cows safely back in the pen. It had taken her and Devin and Chad two days to round them up the first time. She knew if the cows had gotten out to the far pasture, it would have taken them a lot longer to convince them to come back.

"Good job, Leanne," George said as she sat, her breath shaky, her pulse still pounding.

She acknowledged his rare compliment with a duck of her head, then grabbed her horse's reins and turned back toward the herd.

"What are you doing?" Reuben called out.

"Getting these cows processed." Time was wasting. George would be furious as it was, no sense making him angrier.

"No. You need to get your bearings. Your horse needs to rest a moment. Shift its mindset."

Leanne fought down frustration that she hadn't thought of that. Though her horse was breathing heavily, she knew the run hadn't worn it out. But it had put it in a racing frame of mind, as Reuben had said. She needed to settle it down.

So she nodded her acknowledgment of what he said, pulled in another breath and exerted a gentle but steady pressure on the reins to hold her horse in. He seemed to understand what she wanted and stopped its prancing and shifting, settling down and lowering its head.

Reuben brought his horse alongside hers, talking to it in a low voice, settling it down, as well.

Up until now Leanne's focus had been on the cows, on staying atop her horse, on keeping things under control.

But now that the crisis had been averted, she was far too aware of Reuben beside her, petting his horse, rewarding it, looking as if he hadn't just faced down fifty cow and calf pairs racing for the back of the beyond.

"So what's next?" he asked, shoving his cowboy hat back up his head with the knuckle of his forefinger, giving her a quizzical look.

She fought down a whirl of confusion, letting her old anger with him surface. How could he act so casual? As if they hadn't shared so much? Been through so much?

"What are you doing here?" she blurted out.

He looked taken aback, but then his features hardened, reflecting her own churning emotions.

"I came to say goodbye."

"You're leaving?" She shouldn't be surprised. It was what he did best. "What about the arena?"

"I told Cord he needed to find someone else to do the assessment." His horse did a turn away, restless now, but Reuben got it turned to face the cows. In the process he ended up even closer to Leanne and her horse.

"Why are you here?" George called out, joining them.

"So nice to be made welcome," Reuben muttered, his jaw clenched. He turned to his father. "Like I was saying to Leanne, I just stopped in to say goodbye and came into the middle of this mess."

"Sure. Yeah." George turned away from him and back to Leanne. "Chad is still here.

Guess we should get going." He walked away from them, heading back to the head gate.

Leanne nodded, trying hard not to look at her watch. She had told Shauntelle to drop Austin off at suppertime. If it were only her and Chad and George, sorting these cows would take longer.

"You can't do this alone."

Reuben's tone rubbed her completely wrong. So full of authority. But his words were, unfortunately, correct.

"Done it before," she snapped. "Can do it again."

"Not without Devin."

She didn't need to be reminded of that particular betrayal. Though she didn't blame the kid, it was still lousy timing on Devin's part that he quit right now. This was only the first batch of cows they needed to work through. In the coming week they needed to get the rest of the cows down off the upper pastures, process and wean them. On top of that, she had committed to taking minutes at a meeting of the Rodeo Group. She had too much to do and not enough help to do it now that Devin was gone.

But she wasn't going to admit that to Reuben.

She turned to him, fighting a confusing

mix of anger and loss as she held his dark brown eyes. Eyes she had once found herself lost in.

Focus. He's not the man you thought he was.

"So I guess this is goodbye," she said, turning away from him, determined not to let him see how he affected her. "I need to get to work."

"Not on your own."

"What do you propose I do? Run to the hired-hand store?" She couldn't keep the snappy tone out of her voice.

She'd heard nothing for the past three years from this man. A man she had given her heart to and so much more.

And now he swoops back into her life and tells her what she should and shouldn't do on a ranch he walked away from? A ranch he never showed any interest in?

"I could help out until you're done," he said.

All she could do was stare at him. Reuben? Working alongside her on the ranch?

She shook her head. "No. That's not happening. We'll manage on our own."

"You won't and you know it," he returned. It wasn't too hard to hear the annoyance in his voice.

Well, she didn't care. He had no right to be frustrated with her.

Leanne closed her eyes, trying to bring her focus back to what needed to be done and how she could swing it.

She couldn't have him around. She didn't want to live in the past with its pain and resentment. She wanted to move on.

Then she heard the jangle of his horse's bit and when she opened her eyes again he was already moving his horse into the herd, calling out to George.

"How many do you want at a time?"

"Send me ten pairs," George was saying. "But don't get too fussed if cows and calves get separated."

A chill shot through her as she heard George give Reuben directions.

"I don't think we need his help," she called out to George, anger blending with fear.

"Too late," Reuben tossed over his shoulder. "I'm not going anywhere until this job is done."

Chapter Three

"Send them through now, Reuben. Keep them moving."

Reuben ignored his father's barked commands and pushed the last of the cows into the pen keeping his horse right behind the last cow. He nodded for Chad to shut the gate. The poor guy looked exhausted, but then so did Leanne. She was slouched in her saddle now, wiping her face with a hanky. She had lost her hat in the race to get ahead of the cows. Her hair hung in a lank ponytail down her back, loose strands sticking to her flushed face.

"Chad, come over here and help me get these cows done," his father called out.

Reuben leaned on his saddle, watching poor Chad clambering over the fence and joining his father on the walkway to help finish needling the cows. Beyond them, in the second, much-larger pen, the cows and calves were finally settled, munching on the hay. Once the rest of the cows were through, the work was done for the day.

He arched his back, working out a kink, then slowly dismounted. He was going to feel every single muscle in his hips and legs tomorrow. He hadn't ridden in years and yet was surprised how quickly the old skills came back.

Leanne got off her horse, as well. She slipped the reins over the horse's head then walked her horse toward him.

Her expression was guarded as she trudged through the pen. Once again he struggled with her angry reaction to his presence. Where did that come from and what right did she have to be upset with him? She was the one who had betrayed him. Marrying his brother while he was giving her the space she said she needed.

"This is just the first bunch?" he asked as she joined him, her horse heaving a heavy sigh as if the day had been too long for him, as well.

"Yeah. We've got eighty more head up in the higher pastures."

"Shouldn't this have been done a month ago?" he asked, stretching his neck. "Time isn't on your side."

"We've been fortunate." Her voice held an edge of tension, which annoyed him.

"Considering your main hand just quit, I wouldn't say that."

"It's a glitch," she snapped.

"So you figure on gathering them tomorrow?"

"I can't. Your father and I have a meeting with the Cedar Ridge Rodeo Group tomorrow. It will have to wait until Friday."

"The weather is only going to cooperate so long," he said, struggling to keep his frustration down.

"I checked the forecast. We have a week of good weather ahead of us." The anger in her voice wasn't hard to miss.

"I'm trying to help," he said.

"Now?" Leanne's eyes narrowed. Then she seemed to gather her emotions. "I'm sorry. I appreciate what you just did."

He just nodded, realizing from the tension in her voice how difficult the apology was for her.

"I couldn't very well leave you hanging."

Reuben led his horse through a gate on the far side of the pen, trying to ignore his father's yelling at Chad.

"How many ranch hands have you been

through in the past year?" he asked, opening the gate so she could lead her horse through.

Leanne's only reply was a halfhearted shrug. Which told him they'd probably been through a few.

He wanted to push the issue but he had already said enough. Besides, what did it matter to him what Leanne and his father were doing or the difficulties they were having? It wasn't his ranch and he had no skin in the game.

You should stay. Help.

On the heels of that thought came Leanne's anger with him. Why should he deal with that on purpose?

Daylight was waning by the time the horses were unbridled and released into their own pasture.

Leanne closed the door of the tack shed and arched her back, her eyes closed.

"You look beat," Reuben said, feeling a touch of concern.

"Just another day in paradise," she quipped. Then she walked over to a bale of hay and was about to fork some to the horses when Reuben stopped her. "I'll take care of that."

She nodded her thanks, then without another word to him walked toward where George and Chad stood. Reuben stabbed the fork into the hay bale, fighting his annoyance with her attitude. As if she had any right to be so cool with him.

Chad was cleaning up the syringes and George looked up when he joined them. "Good work" was all he said, but coming from George, that was high praise. Then he turned to Leanne. "Is Austin in the house?"

"Shauntelle texted me a few minutes ago. She just put him to bed but she brought supper. She's waiting at the house until I can leave."

"You go then, Leanne. We'll be right here," George said, then he glanced over at Reuben. "You should join us for supper. I'm sure Shauntelle made enough."

He heard Leanne's swift intake of breath but he didn't bother looking her way, sensing he would see the same anger he had when he first came. Her reaction made him want to turn down the invitation, but the fact that his father had asked was a small acknowledgment of Reuben's presence. A few crumbs tossed his way from his dad.

And right about now, he was ready to take something, anything, away from this visit. If it wasn't from Leanne then it may as well be from his father.

"Sure. That sounds good," he said.

"You can wash up in the house," George

said, then turned to Chad. “When you’re done here, you can go home.” Then George walked away, leaving Chad with syringes and empty bottles to clean up.

“How long have you been working for my father?” Reuben asked Chad, who was gathering up the syringes and dumping them into a large plastic tub for cleaning.

“Few days. Not long.”

“You ever work on a ranch before?”

Chad slowly shook his head, looking apprehensive. “No. But I need the work. Got a family to take care of.”

“You ride at all?”

“I’m willing to learn.”

Reuben held the man’s eyes, sensing the desperation in them. He’d have to be at the end of his rope to want to put up with his father’s abuse for the sake of a job.

However Reuben didn’t give the poor guy another week. Chad seemed like a decent fellow but he needed someone who was able to take the time to help him out and show him the ropes. George would never be that guy. Leanne might, but he guessed any extra time she might have was taken up with Austin.

There was no way they could keep this ranch going.

This isn’t your problem, he reminded himself. *You're on your way out of here. Stick to your plan.*

But as he walked back to the house, George and Leanne walking ahead of him, he couldn't shake the idea that the Bar W's time was done.

George and Leanne really needed to sell the place.

"So this job of yours. What will you do?" George was asking Reuben.

"I'll be contracting for a large engineering firm," Reuben replied, his voice even and measured in spite of the antagonism in George's voice. "This job will get me opportunities all around the world."

Leanne concentrated on her food, exhaustion clawing at her. The day had been emotionally and physically taxing. Devin's quitting had created a huge problem she wasn't ready to deal with. And while Reuben's help was appreciated, his presence wasn't.

She couldn't deal with all this right now. She wanted nothing more than to retreat to her room, but she was determined not to let Reuben know how much he got to her.

"I can see why you'd like that job. Moving around. Just like you've always lived," George put in, annoyance edging his voice as he scooped up some of the casserole Shauntelle had dropped off.

Leanne had never been so happy to see her friend. She wanted to fall into her arms, tell her all her current struggles, but she couldn't. Only Tabitha knew Leanne's secrets, and her sister had been so busy the past couple of days that Leanne hadn't had a chance to connect with her.

"Dirk liked staying in one place," George continued. "He would have stuck around. Helped on the ranch."

In spite of her own frustration with him, Leanne felt a touch of sympathy for Reuben. As long as she'd known Dirk and Reuben, it was obvious George favored the son of his first wife. His beloved Joelle.

Didn't matter what Reuben accomplished, it was either wrong or not as good as anything Dirk did. After Dirk died, George grew more bitter, railing against everyone and everything and, for some reason, Reuben most of all.

"So where is this amazing job based?" George continued.

"California. The company has contracts all over the world," Reuben said, pushing his food around his plate. "It's a great opportunity. A chance to make good money and be independent. And travel."

Leanne shouldn't have been surprised that Reuben would take this job. His constant moving around had been one of those important issues they had planned to discuss when they decided they would be together. She had hoped he would come and work on the ranch, but Reuben had been adamant that his father would never want him back or give him any share in the Bar W. Dirk was the favored son, he would be the one inheriting and Reuben had no desire to put himself through more humiliation.

"And no more rodeo?" his father asked.

Reuben glanced over at Leanne just as she looked at him. She ducked her head, focusing on the plate in front of her.

Leanne was thankful that in spite of George's antagonism to Reuben, he carried the conversation. She couldn't make idle chitchat with a man who had let her down so badly. Treated her so poorly.

A man she'd thought, at one time, she would be spending the rest of her life with.

And right now, sitting with him only a few feet away, with Austin sleeping upstairs, her own feelings were in such turmoil, she wasn't sure what she would say to him.

"Well, whatever works," George said, taking a drink of his water. "You're not in a saddle anymore but you're still running around, aren't you?"

"Haven't found a reason to settle down yet." Then Reuben turned to Leanne. "This is a great supper. Thanks so much for having me."

His polite smile and impersonal comment created a clench of dismay that surprised and frustrated her. All through the meal he'd been unfailingly polite, asking George questions about the ranch, the hired hands, the community. He didn't bother asking anything of her.

Or about Austin, which cut deepest of all.

"You're welcome," she said, keeping her voice cool. "It was the least we could do after you helped us out."

He shot her a frown, clearly picking up on the faint note of sarcasm that had crept into her voice.

"It was the right thing to do. So what are you going to do now that Devin has quit?" Reuben asked, his gaze fixed on Leanne, as if daring her to answer his question.

Leanne glanced at George, who glowered, tapping his fingers on the table.

"I don't know," George said finally. "Sometimes I think we should let it all go." Then he glanced at Leanne. "But then I think of Austin and know we should keep going."

His words created a low-level panic in her.

Though Leanne knew, when it came right down to it, her father-in-law would never sell the ranch, he had floated the idea a couple of times. And she had simply let him talk, hoping he would change his mind.

He always did.

"We'll keep going," she said, giving George an encouraging smile. "We'll advertise for another hand. That's how we got Devin and he knew his stuff." She didn't add the fact that George had been the one to drive him to quit, but she lived in hope that they would find someone who was able to ignore George's bluster and do the work.

"This Chad guy. Where did you find him?" Reuben asked.

"Word of mouth," Leanne said, glancing over at George who had gone quiet, staring off into the middle distance. Leanne caught him doing this more often the past while. As if he was ruminating on life. Looking back into a past he couldn't change and the losses that had caused him so much pain.

"He seems like a good guy, but not too experienced," Reuben said.

"He'll learn."

"But you're still shorthanded. And you've got a lot of work ahead of you getting the rest of the cows processed and the calves weaned."

Leanne was wondering why he was giving her the third degree. What did he care about what was happening on the ranch? He never had cared about it before.

Or about other things.

"We are shorthanded," George said to Reuben, jumping into the conversation. "But you could help us out. You said you don't have to go back for a couple of weeks. You could help Leanne get the cows down from the upper pastures. Help us wean them."

"We can find someone else," Leanne chimed in. There was no way she could handle Reuben being at the ranch all day. "And besides, Reuben said he was leaving town."

"I can stay, help out around here," Reuben said.

Leanne could only stare at him. "Why?"

"My dad asked if I could, and I can," Reuben said, his tone even. Measured. As if he was challenging her. "And I know you won't find anyone to help on the ranch on such short notice."

Leanne pressed her lips together, struggling for self-control. She was the new secretary of the Rodeo Group. And when she'd found out Reuben would be doing the assessment on the arena, she figured it would only require seeing him for a couple of meetings and then he would be done.

But to have him here? Every day?

"Good. Then that's settled," George said. "We'll see you on Friday."

Leanne felt a headache crawling up her neck and had suddenly had enough of trying to sit through this visit. Trying to be polite to a man who had once held her heart and, instead, had pushed her away when she needed him most.

She couldn't struggle through inane conversation with Reuben for a single minute longer.

"Excuse me," she mumbled, shooting a glance at George, her eyes barely grazing over Reuben. She picked up her plate and carried it to the kitchen. She set her plate on the counter, gripping the edge as she tried to keep it together. In spite of her anger with Reuben, she was still disappointed to see how much he affected her. After all he had done, or rather hadn't done, he could still make her heart tremble. At one time in her life, she would have prayed about this visit, asking God to give her strength. But she hadn't attended church since Dirk died. The burdens on her shoulders weighed too heavily.

And now it looked like he would be here

on the ranch. Every day until they were done moving and weaning.

She drew in a deep breath, then began scraping the food off the plate into the garbage can.

"Not going to feed those to Buster? I'm sure the old dog would love those leftovers."

Ruben's deep voice behind her made her jump. Why didn't he stay in the dining room? She just wanted this evening over and him gone.

"Buster's not around anymore," she said.

"What? Since when?"

"He died shortly after Austin was born." In spite of her feelings toward him, she softened her voice as she gave him the news. Though the old collie had been the ranch's dog, he had always been attached to Reuben and was always right at his heels everywhere he went.

"I was wondering where he was when we were working with the cows. I thought he was sleeping. Figured he was probably pretty old." Reuben released a heavy sigh as he set the bowls with the leftover food on the counter.

She didn't imagine the sorrow in his voice, and for the smallest moment she wanted to reach out to him and console him. But she stopped herself. He didn't deserve her pity.

George came into the kitchen, setting the last of the plates beside the sink.

"If you don't mind, I'm turning in," he said to Leanne. "Tell Shauntelle thanks for dinner."

He turned to Reuben. "So we'll see you again?"

Reuben nodded, then George left, his footsteps slow as he walked through the kitchen to the stairs leading to his bedroom in his wing of the house.

Reuben waited until he was gone, then turned back to Leanne. "He looks tired," he said, his voice quiet.

"He's getting older and he hasn't been feeling well lately." Leanne kept her tone conversational, wishing Reuben would just leave. She wanted nothing more than to go to her own bedroom, crawl into bed, pull the covers over her head and end this day. But she plugged on.

"Why does he keep going?" Reuben asked. "Why doesn't he sell this place? Sounds like he's talked about it."

"Sell the place?" Leanne couldn't keep the incredulous tone out of her voice as she finished loading the dishwasher. "This place has been in the Walsh family for generations. He can't do that. He *won't* do that," she amended.

Reuben gave her a surprised look. "You seem bothered by the idea."

"You don't sell land," she said, closing the dishwasher and punching the buttons, his nearness creating unwelcome feelings countered by his casual dismissal of everything she now held dear. "I can't believe you would even say that. You, a Walsh."

"C'mon, Leanne. Be realistic," Reuben said, frowning his puzzlement as he ignored her last statement. "It's just you and my dad now, and Chad who is a nice guy but no cowhand. And knowing my father, you've been through more than a few hired hands already. You can't keep going like this."

"I'm capable," she countered, leaning back against the counter, her arms folded in a defensive gesture over her chest. "I've spent the last three years learning how to handle cows, drive a tractor, work a horse. Prove my worth to your father. I can manage the work."

"I don't know why you would want to get into my father's good graces," Reuben said with a harsh laugh. "Those four years you and Dirk were engaged, my dad would have nothing to do with you. He fought with Dirk all the time about his dating you. And now you're working with him like he's a partner you can trust. How do you know he won't change his mind and cut you out?"

Leanne felt again the sting of that old rejection. When she was dating Dirk, she knew George's disapproval was one of the reasons Dirk kept putting off setting a wedding date. Dirk kept telling her it would take time and that he wanted everything to be just right before they got married. But he hung on for four long years, giving her excuse after excuse.

She finally broke up with him, realizing that it was probably for the best.

Because no matter how she had tried to convince herself that Dirk—safe solid secure Dirk—was the better man, it was the wild and unpredictable Reuben who had always held her heart.

And for a few blissful weeks, after she broke up with Dirk and she and Reuben found each other at that wedding in Costa Rica, she thought she had finally found her heart's true home.

Foolish, stupid, trusting girl.

But she was here now. Reuben was her past. Austin was her present and future. He was her focus now. Not this man who broke his promises to her and broke her heart.

"Land is an inheritance. A legacy. It's security," she said, repeating all the reasons she had dated Dirk. "You don't give that up."

"Security always was important to you, wasn't it?" Reuben's voice held a hard edge. "That's why you stayed with Dirk so long. That's why you went running back to him the first chance you could. After I thought we had shared something unique. Something I'd never had with anyone before."

His words dug into her heart, resurrecting feelings she thought she had dealt with, but the dismissive and furious tone of his voice stripped them all away. Laying bare the selfish man he truly was.

She felt her hands curl into fists and for a moment she wanted to hit him. Strike at him. Lash out in pain and fury and hurt.

"Dirk at least stood by me," Leanne said, pulling in a long, slow breath, trying to still her pounding heart, the old, painful tightness gripping her tired head. Always a sign of stress and sorrow. "He helped me when I needed him, which is more than I can say for you."

Silence followed this remark and she wondered what he would say to that. If he would now finally admit to what he had done. Or hadn't done.

"I wish I had even the smallest inkling of

what you're talking about" was all he said, sounding genuinely puzzled.

All she could do was stare at him.

"Are you delusional or are you really that insensitive?" How could he act as if he had no clue of what had happened between them? Did he think she would just forget those panicked text messages she had sent and his harsh, hard replies telling her to leave him alone? That he didn't want to have anything to do with her anymore?

"What's really going on, Leanne?" Reuben asked as she busied herself putting the leftovers away. "I can't believe you feel you have any right to be angry with me. Why?"

Where to start?

Leanne snapped covers on the leftovers and shoved them into the refrigerator, giving herself a chance to ease the fury clawing at her heart. She had told herself repeatedly that she was over this man and he didn't deserve one minute of her thoughts.

"Doesn't matter," she snapped. What she and Reuben had was past and gone. He'd had his chance and he'd tossed it away. That he would be working here was an inconvenience she would simply have to deal with until he was gone. Because if there was one thing she knew about Reuben, it was that his departure was inevitable.

"But it does matter. If we'll be working together for a while, I'd like us to not be circling each other." Then, to her dismay, he took a step closer to her and in spite of her obvious anger with him, he touched her shoulder. It was nothing more than the whisper of his hand over her shirt, but it was as if sparks flew from his fingertips.

She clung to the door of the refrigerator, as if to regain her balance, then turned to him.

"Why does this matter now? Why didn't it matter three years ago?"

"It did matter. What we had was everything to me. When we got together in Costa Rica, I thought we had finally come to the place you and I should have been years earlier. Instead you deserted me and ran to Dirk and married him."

All she could do was stare at him. "Deserted you? How… Where…" She shook her head, trying to settle her confusion. "You were the one who did the leaving. I sent you text after text and all I got from you was rejection." The old hurt spiraled up and she had to fight down the pain and, to her humiliation, the tears.

"Rejection? Texts? I have no idea what you're talking about."

The puzzlement on his face was almost her undoing. He seemed genuinely disconcerted.

"I feel like there's this gap between us I don't know how to bridge," he said.

Then, to her dismay, he took that one step separating them and fingered a strand of hair away from her face. She closed her eyes, her own emotions in flux. Her hand twitched at her side, longing to come up and cover his. To reconnect with someone she couldn't forget.

But then she heard Austin cry out and she was doused with icy reality.

"I should go check on him," she said, moving away from him.

"Can I come with you? I haven't seen him yet today."

His casual request was like an arrow in her heart. How could he act this way around Austin? How could he simply relegate him to one corner of his life? Like he didn't matter?

Her indignation and frustrated fury with him rose up. But behind that came a quiet question.

Maybe if he saw Austin face-to-face again he might relent. Maybe seeing him again would make a difference.

Really? If seeing him yesterday hadn't, why would it now?

Her mind did battle with herself as she recalled his coldhearted texts of rejection. The replies she typed out with trembling fingers on her cell phone, alone, pregnant and uncertain of her future.

"Please?" he asked, the pleading note in his voice easing away her resistance.

"Of course you can," she said, determined to be an adult about this, tossing out one last-ditch effort to make him own up to his responsibilities. "He's your son after all."

Chapter Four

Her words hung between them, echoing in the silent kitchen. Soft-spoken, but they rocked his soul. He felt like he was fifteen years old again and being tossed off the dock at Cedar Lake. Suspended in the air in disbelief, wondering what it would feel like when he went in.

"My son?" He choked the words out.

"Yes. Austin is your son," she said, her words sounded like they came from far away.

"My son?" he repeated, feeling like an idiot.

"I know I could keep him from you and not let you see him. That would be what you deserve, but I'm trying to take the moral high ground here. After all, you'll be here every day. You can't avoid him the entire time."

Reuben stared at her, trying to catch up one

word, one phrase at a time as he surfaced to the truth.

"What are you saying? What do you mean?"

Leanne glared at him, eyes narrowed. "Please do me a favor and stop acting so surprised."

"But I am." He struggled to settle the information, his mind ticking back, trying to think, to organize thoughts he couldn't pin down.

"I don't know why you are," she snapped. "This certainly isn't news to you. I still can't believe how casual you've been about the whole thing. You came flying onto the ranch and when you saw him, you acted like he was just some other kid, like he was—"

"My nephew," he interrupted. "Which he is. Dirk's son." Why was she saying Austin was his son? If that was true, why hadn't she told him before? Why wait until now?

Leanne shook her head, and her narrowed eyes latched on to him. "He's not Dirk's. He's yours. The same kid I told you about over three years ago. The same kid you told me you didn't want to have anything to do with."

He held his hands up, still trying to absorb what she was saying. "Whoa, what do you mean, I didn't want to have anything to do with him? This is the first I've heard about this."

"How can you look me straight in the eye and lie like that?"

"I'm not lying. How…when…" He caught himself. "Let's back up here. You got pregnant. Are you saying—"

"It happened at your cousin's wedding. The 'mistake' we both agreed we had made," she made sarcastic air quotes, hooking the air with her fingers.

He could only stare at her, trying to digest all this.

"You got pregnant then?"

"Yes. Except I didn't know at the time, obviously. And then we decided we needed to think about what we were doing and the repercussions of what we had done—"

"You were the one who wanted space and time," he interrupted, struggling to follow where she was leading, his frustration edging into his voice. "I was all for keeping in touch. For making a commitment right then and there but you wanted to talk to Dirk first. But he was gone to Europe. When we came back, I respected that space and distance while you waited. I let you have your time alone and didn't bug you."

She held her hand up as if to stop anything else he might say. "And obviously you seemed to think that extended to responding callously to my texts when I told you I was pregnant."

"What? When? I didn't get any texts."

"I tried to phone you a bunch of times the night I found out but you didn't answer and I got sent to voice mail," she said, her arms wrapped around her waist, eyes narrowed in fury. "I was so distraught. So upset when I found out. Dirk was on his way back from Europe and I hadn't had a chance to tell him about us. So I sent you a text instead to tell you about Austin and that you were the father. And when you finally texted me back you told me that you were sorry but you couldn't take this on. That I was on my own." She spat the words out at him like venom. "I asked you if you were serious. You replied that you were and that you didn't want to have anything more to do with me. That you felt guilty about being with me. That I should go back to Dirk. That he was the better person." She listed off the reasons in a voice that both cut and accused simultaneously. "Then you told me not to contact you anymore. Then you blocked me. Or something. I never heard from you again."

"I would remember if I'd had that conversation. And I would never have said anything like that." He dug back into his memory, feeling as if his entire world had been shaken, unable to believe she would think this of him. "I was waiting for you to talk to Dirk so we could be together." If he had known he was a father on top of all that, he would have come charging back to Cedar Ridge immediately to make things right.

"Don't act so confused. I saw the answers you sent me. I even showed them to Tabitha because I couldn't believe you would say what you did. And she helpfully reminded me of other times when you were irresponsible."

"What other times?"

"You said you were going to take me to prom and you bailed on me. Then had the nerve to steal a kiss at prom after all."

What? Prom? They were going all the way back to that? Okay, he'd play along, if only to buy time to find his footing. "I didn't take you to prom because Dirk told me to back off. That you were his girlfriend."

"It wasn't true. Dirk and I had broken up."

"Just like you and Dirk had broken up before you came to Costa Rica?" He couldn't wrap his head around all of this.

"I broke up with him that time and you needn't look so surprised."

"That's all beside the point and in the past."

"Maybe, but to me it's all part and parcel of

who you are. You don't keep your promises. And don't tell me it isn't true. You're bailing on the Rodeo Group."

In spite of his confusion and frustration with the information she had just dumped on him, Reuben knew how his quitting the Rodeo Group looked to her.

But he wasn't about to tell her it was because being around her and her unreasoning anger made it difficult for him.

"Never mind that. You need to know that I didn't get any of those texts you're talking about," he repeated.

"You can't argue with what I saw on my phone and what my sister saw. We can argue about the texts all we want, but the reality of it all is, whether you want to admit it or not, Austin is your son."

He felt like he was stuck in some maze trying to find his way out.

"Do you still have the texts?" It was a dumb question, but right now dumb was all he could manage.

She looked away, shaking her head. "I deleted them. It was too hurtful to keep the reminder of..." She paused, her voice breaking. Then she held her head up, eyes blazing at him. "It was the hardest thing I ever had to deal with. I felt alone and betrayed by you."

Reuben didn't know how else to tell her that he hadn't received any messages from her. "Okay. We can resolve this fast. I'll check." He pulled his phone out of his pocket, thumbed it on and hit the messages icon.

He scrolled through his message contacts, and as he did so, he realized something else and he stopped.

"Well? Did you find them?" Her voice was like ice.

He lowered his phone, pulling in a deep, heavy sigh as he shook his head. "I won't find them. I lost that phone and everything on it and I forgot to back it up."

"That's convenient."

"As convenient as your marriage to Dirk was, apparently," he snapped.

Leanne sucked in her breath. "That's a low blow."

"So was finding out that, after we had decided to make a commitment to each other, after we realized we should have been together from the beginning, you couldn't wait to marry Dirk when you got back home."

"I didn't have a choice," she said. "I was alone. Pregnant. I had no place to go. No job. No options. You had pushed me away. Rejected me—"

"According to you," he interrupted, refusing to allow her to shove him into that role.

"Dirk came back from Europe the day after I got your texts and told me he was sorry," she carried on, ignoring his interjection. "He begged me to take him back. He said he wanted to marry me right away. That he didn't care what his father thought. I had to tell him the truth about the baby. He was angry with me, but he didn't change his mind. I was scared and confused, and I could only think of my baby. So I said yes. He was being so kind and considerate. We flew to Vegas and got married right away. We had our honeymoon there. And you know what happened on our drive home from the airport." Her voice broke, and in spite of his frustration and confusion, he reached out to her.

But she pulled away.

They stood that way, staring at each other, at a stalemate.

"You're an engineer," she said, stone faced. "If you are still in doubt about Austin's parentage, you can do the math. Austin was born eight and a half months after Dirk and I got married. I think George assumed he was early when, in fact, Austin was overdue."

That still didn't prove anything to him. For all he knew, she had been intimate with Dirk before he and Leanne had gone to the wedding in Costa Rica, but he wasn't bringing that up right now.

"And I can see by the look on your face that you still doubt me." She shook her head in disgust. "You think Austin might be Dirk's child."

"It's a possibility" was all he could say in his defense.

"Why would I lie about this? How would it benefit me? George thinks Austin is Dirk's son. We both know what he thinks of you."

Which didn't precisely help her cause.

"So why haven't you told George the truth if Austin is, indeed, my son?"

Leanne's eyes flicked away from him and a flush tinged her cheeks. Which only underlined his assumptions.

"Dirk made me promise," she said, her voice quiet. "Just before the accident, on our way home from the airport, he made me promise not to tell George the truth about Austin. It was the last thing he said to me before—"

"Before the accident," he said.

She nodded and was about to say more when Austin started crying again and she hurried away, as if glad of the distraction.

Reuben followed behind her, walking more

slowly, still digesting everything she had thrown at him. If she had felt alone and abandoned, of course she would've turned to Dirk.

But he hadn't abandoned her, he reminded himself as he trudged up the stairs. Clearly more was going on here, and right now he couldn't put everything together from what she had told him.

Austin was sitting up in his bed, crying in the darkness of his room.

Leanne hurried inside, dropped on his bed and pulled him close, her one hand cradling his head. "It's okay, honey. I'm here. Did you have a bad dream?"

"I scared," he said. "I scared of da horse."

"It's okay, sweetie," Leanne said, as he crawled onto her lap, slipping his chubby arms around her neck. "You don't have to be scared. I'm here."

Austin looked over her shoulder. "Uncle Wooben," he said with a note of surprise.

"Hey, buddy." Reuben stayed in the doorway, watching as Leanne brushed the little boy's hair back from his face, studying the boy's features, trying to find any resemblance.

His hair was auburn like Leanne's. His eyes brown.

Like his.

Or like George's.

"You come here," Austin demanded, suddenly not so sad anymore.

Reuben pushed himself away from the door frame, glancing around the darkened room as his eyes adjusted to the gloom.

This had been his room when he'd lived here. All traces of him were gone, however. All his awards, ribbons and plaques from competitions he'd entered and won.

Instead, cute prints now hung on the painted walls. A toy box was tucked at the end of the bed. A small rocking horse that Uncle Boyce had made for Reuben still sat in the corner of the room. One tiny remaining claim he could make on the house.

He was surprised his father had kept it.

"Come. Sit," Austin said.

Reuben hesitated, still not sure what to think of this child and where to put him in his life. Sure he'd known about Austin. The child had always been a reminder to him of Leanne's betrayal and her need for security. For Dirk.

"Come here," Austin said again.

It would look silly to keep standing there, so Reuben walked over to the bed, perching on the edge.

Austin grinned at him, his teeth flashing white in the half dark and Reuben grinned back.

He was a cute kid, that was for sure, but to him he was simply that. A cute kid.

Then Austin angled his head down and Reuben saw what he hadn't yesterday. A tiny, lighter patch of hair swirling out of the cowlick on the top of Austin's head. It wasn't large. You'd have to pay attention to see it.

But it was the same light patch of hair his mother had. The same patch of hair he had.

He felt his world shift yet again as the evidence in front of him, combined with Leanne's insistence, gave him proof he could no longer deny. Austin truly was his son.

His gaze shifted to hers. The look on her face showed him that she had seen his reaction.

Reuben reached down and fingered the patch of Austin's lighter hair, as if touching it would make it real. "My mom always colored her hair, but she had the same bit of differently colored hair" was all he could say, a confusing rush of feelings overwhelming him. "So do I. My mom told me it was hereditary. That her dad had it too."

Leanne said nothing as a heavy silence fell between them.

Then he looked up at her, still trying to sort everything out. "I don't know what to say."

Leanne's expression softened.

"So, do you believe me now?"

"I do. I have to."

"I'm sad that it took such hard proof. I was hoping you would have taken my word for truth."

He fought down a beat of frustration. Surely she had to understand he would have some doubts? But she seemed to think that he'd known and rejected her.

He blew out his breath, looking down at Austin again who was now yawning. Reuben crouched down, as if seeing him in an entirely new light. His son. He and Leanne truly did have a son. They were now bound with an unbreakable, undeniable bond.

And what are you going to do about that? Can you still leave?

Leanne pulled Austin close against her, tucking his head under her chin. As he watched Leanne holding Austin, remnants of dreams he and Leanne had spun those two weeks in Costa Rica returned.

The two of them, living on a ranch somewhere. Leanne had imagined it to be the Bar

W ranch because she wanted their children raised in the same place he was. Reuben had said he wanted to live anywhere but the Bar W. They hadn't exactly fought about it—they were too in love at the time—but it had caused a moment of tension.

And now, here she was, raising Austin on a ranch with no future that he could see, clinging to it for Austin's sake.

Then Leanne lowered Austin onto his bed, tucking the sheets around him and brushing a kiss over his forehead. "Good night, sweetheart," she whispered. Austin curled up on his side, grinning at Reuben. "Good night, Uncle Wooben," he said.

Reuben gave him a forced smile, then left the room as Leanne switched on a nightlight. Then she closed the door behind her and led the way down the stairs back to the kitchen. She stopped there and turned to him. "So. That's your son."

"He's a cute kid" was all he could manage. "I forgot to give him his present."

"So, are you still leaving in a couple of weeks?" she asked.

Her question hung between them, unspoken ones hovering behind it.

"I don't know." One thing he knew for sure was that, in spite of his father's surprising request for help, he was moving on to that job. It was the opportunity of a lifetime as his future boss Marshall had said, and Reuben knew he was right.

She sighed heavily, which clearly told him what she thought of his evasive answer. "Okay. Then we'll play the situation by ear for now. And I guess you'll be coming here for the next few days."

"I'll be here until the cows are brought home and weaned," he said. "I know you need the help. Besides, how can I refuse my own father's request?" He couldn't keep the faintly bitter note out of his voice.

Leanne sighed lightly, resting her hands on a chair tucked into a corner nook of the kitchen. "I know you don't want to be here, and quite frankly I'm not crazy about your being here either, but for now we'll have to find a way to work together."

Reuben looked around the house he'd lived in for years and eased out a heavy sigh as echoes of old fights with George rose up and mocked him.

"You don't like it here, do you?" Leanne asked.

"It's my childhood home, but it doesn't hold lots of happy memories." He turned to her. "You always loved it here, though."

She nodded, a faint smile playing around her lips as she looked around the house. The first he'd seen since he arrived. That it was thoughts of the ranch causing it shouldn't surprise him. "I couldn't imagine why anyone would ever want to leave here," she said. "A place with roots and history."

Reuben knew firsthand how much she loved the ranch and wanted to be involved in it. Even when she and Dirk had dated, she'd learned to ride a horse so she could help with pasture moves and gathering cows. Dirk wasn't as enamored of the ranch as she was, and when she wanted him to teach her how to run the tractor, he'd refused. So she finagled Reuben into doing it. She was a natural, he had said, and then, of course, Dirk was jealous that Reuben had spent the time with Leanne instead of him.

"Depends on what type of history you have," he said, thinking of George and the treatment he'd doled out. He shoved his hand through his hair in frustration as he thought of the young boy upstairs. A child he had always thought of as his nephew and now had to think of as his son. "And no matter what you think of me, you have to admit I didn't have the best example of fatherhood."

"Are you saying you don't want to be a father to Austin?"

He easily heard the pain in her voice and he knew, once again, he had gone about this all wrong. He closed his eyes, praying for the right words, praying to a God he hadn't spent a lot of time with in the past. A God he had only recently come back to.

"I'm saying that I'm not sure how good a father I can be. George's blood runs through my veins too. And we both know what kind of a father he was."

"So you'll stick around to help with the cows but then you're gone? Leaving your son behind?" Her fists were clenched at her sides, her eyes narrowed, her voice hard.

Her anger was like a wave, beating at him, dragging at the foundation of his life.

Please, Lord. Help me out here.

He forced himself to hold her angry gaze, drawing back into himself, pushing aside what Leanne wanted and what he wanted.

"I'm saying that I have to make the best decision for Austin's sake," he finally said.

She held his eyes a moment, then seemed to relax. "I'm sorry. You're right."

Then she dragged her hands over her face, her weariness suddenly apparent.

"You look tired," he said. "You should go to bed and I should leave."

"Thanks again for your help," she said, giving him a ghost of a smile. She hesitated a moment as if she wanted to say more. He wasn't sure what else there was to say right now.

Then she turned and walked away, heading back up the stairs that led to her wing of the house. He watched her go, then left himself, his footsteps echoing in the cavernous kitchen. Outside, the quiet and darkness seemed to enfold him.

The wide swath of stars overhead caught his attention. He looked up at the night sky and, in spite of everything that had happened, he smiled. He hadn't seen the stars like this in years. Bright, crowded, like a band of sparkling light. He watched them a moment, the utter quiet washing over him. Then, in the distance, he heard the gentle lowing of a cow, the nasal reply from a calf.

To his surprise he was swamped by a wave of homesickness. He had missed this more than he wanted to admit. Missed the silence, the utter majesty of the empty spaces around him. Missed working with his hands, riding horses. Being outside.

He had always known coming back here

to live wasn't a possibility. That it would mean willingly putting up with George's derision and negativity and he knew, much as he needed Reuben now, George would never bring him back into the fold. Give him a share of the ranch.

He stepped into his truck, and as he did, his eyes were drawn to his old room where Austin now slept. The nightlight Leanne had turned on created a soft warm glow though the curtains. His son lay there. His and Leanne's son.

Knowing that made Leanne's marriage to Dirk even more difficult to get past.

Dear Lord, he prayed, *I have no idea what to think or what to do. I'm trusting You'll bring me through this because I'm so confused. I'm afraid of being a father because I don't know how that's supposed to look. I've got too many bad things in my past. I'd never be a good one.*

He let the prayer settle. Then he put his truck in gear and drove away. He would be back tomorrow and a few more tomorrows after that.

And then?

Then he had to go to California and start the life he had carved out for himself.

And Austin? Leanne?

He pushed those thoughts aside. He couldn't deal with that right now.

"So what did he say when you told him?" Tabitha leaned forward, her gaze intent. "Did he finally admit..." Tabitha glanced around the quiet restaurant, then leaned closer in, lowering her voice. "Did he admit the truth?" she asked.

"Only when he saw the lighter patch of hair on Austin's cowlick, the same as he has." Leanne stirred a large spoonful of sugar into her coffee and took a quick sip, resting her elbows on the wooden table tucked into the booth in one corner of Angelo's, one of the local cafés and restaurants in town. Prints of Italy and Venice hung on the walls, an incongruity in the cow town of Cedar Ridge.

"You look tired," Tabitha said, frowning.

"I am. My body aches and my head aches and I'm trying not to feel pressured about getting the cows down before the snow comes."

"There's no snow in the forecast."

Leanne massaged her temples, nodding. "I'm sure hoping they're right for a change. Reuben seemed to think I should be at the ranch today instead of at this meeting." The thought of all she had to do created a low-level panic, but behind that came an annoyance with Reuben.

"You're doing too much," Tabitha said.

"What else am I supposed to do now that Devin quit?"

"Not just with the ranch, honey. I'm also talking about this Rodeo Group you insist on being involved in."

"George asked me to help."

"And what George asks for, George gets."

Leanne chose to ignore the sardonic tone in her sister's voice. Tabitha had her own issues with George, but Leanne refused to make them hers.

"At any rate, it's good for you that Reuben is helping, though that can't be easy for you either."

Leanne sighed again. "Besides giving me advice—too little too late, by the way—he thinks we should sell the ranch."

As she spoke the words aloud, the idea lingered. And for the tiniest of moments she held on to it. Selling the ranch would release her from all the stress she'd been under lately. And the worst of it was, even once the cows were all brought home, the pressure wouldn't ease off. Then it was a matter of trying to find enough feed to get them through the winter and after that it was making sure the bulls got put out on time and after that—

"I can tell you're thinking about it."

Leanne shook her head, as if to dismiss the idea. "I have Austin to think of. The ranch is his security. I simply have to get through all of this. Keep pushing."

"And where does Reuben fit in all of this?"

"Where he did before. In the past."

"But he's Austin's father, and now that he's accepted it—"

"I didn't come here to talk about the ranch or Reuben." Leanne cut her off.

"Your cheeks are flushing though," Tabitha said, in a teasing voice. "He always was a big deal to you."

"Stop. Right now. This isn't simply a high school crush we're talking about." Though even as she denounced her sister's teasing, she had to admit that even the thought of Reuben could ratchet up her heart rate. Just the sight of him brought her back to those two glorious weeks in Costa Rica at his cousin's wedding. When she'd thought they could finally be together.

It had been just a dream.

She shook off the dead-end memories, focusing on her sister and her plans. "So how is work on the clinic coming?" she said, deflecting as quickly as she could. "I drove past to have a look the other day. Looks like the construction is going gangbusters."

"Morgan has been on the internet a lot," Tabitha said. "He wants to make sure his new clinic has all of the best of the best equipment, the latest of the latest." She shook her head in mock dismay. "He is determined to prove he can build and run a vet clinic better than his old boss, Anselm Waters, did." Then Tabitha grinned at her sister. "But I'm guessing you're not that interested in finding out about those fancy new rafters Morgan is ordering."

"I wanted to show support," Leanne said, smiling back at her sister.

"Speaking of. Reuben. If you want I can talk to him. Tell him what a jerk he was."

Leanne shot her a warning glance. "Don't you even think about it. Reuben has had his chance to redeem himself many times and he fell so far from grace, I still haven't heard the echo of the drop at the bottom."

Tabitha made a face, bobbing her head back and forth as if agreeing and yet not. "He admitted Austin was his," she said.

Leanne glanced around, worried someone might overhear. But the only other person in the café was Andy Rodriguez, Shauntelle's father, and he was on his phone.

"You stay away from Reuben. Sure he stepped up but only because I pushed it," Leanne said forcing herself to remember his heartless replies. "You saw those text messages he sent me when I told him I was pregnant. When he told me he didn't want to have anything to do with me. Or 'my kid,' as he so delicately put it."

Tabitha was silent, frowning at her half empty cup of coffee. "You still haven't forgiven him, have you?" Tabitha asked.

"Would you? Ever since I started dating Dirk in high school, Reuben borderline flirted with me. Telling me I was wasting my time with his brother. Constantly paying attention to me even though he knew I was determined to be faithful to Dirk."

"Never mind sneaking that kiss the night of the prom he said he was going to take you to," Tabitha interrupted.

Leanne ignored that comment, the memory of that night still able to create such a mixture of feelings even after all this time. "That kiss was a mistake I still feel guilty about."

"Why? Dirk broke up with you," Tabitha said, her eyes narrowing.

"He came back again."

"I'm sure it was only because he found out about Reuben. Then he waits a couple of years to propose to you, then he keeps you hanging another four years while he works up enough nerve to tell his father he wants to marry a Rennie."

"Well, he finally did," Leanne retorted, feeling she had to stick up for her husband.

"Only after you broke up with him and he took off to France." Tabitha's eyes narrowed, looking thoughtful. "Is there any way Dirk knew about you and Reuben getting together in Costa Rica? Do you think that's the reason he hurried back from his travels in Europe?"

Why was her sister determined to dredge up this old history?

"Doesn't matter if he did. Reuben said he didn't want to marry me and Dirk finally did. That was enough for me. And you don't need to diss my husband. At least he came through, unlike Reuben, who left me hanging in the worst possible way." Leanne stopped there, her cheeks growing even warmer at the resurrection of memories she thought she had dealt with.

Tabitha looked annoyed and Leanne felt bad. She reached across the table and curled her hand around her sister's. "I'm sorry. You're right. I'm just touchy and scared. Seeing Reuben again has been difficult."

"Because of Austin?"

"Partly." Leanne wove her fingers around each other, remembering how being with Reuben affected her. In spite of everything that had happened between them, he could still made her heart race. Could still create that trembling deep in her soul. A feeling she'd never had around Dirk. "I want everything done. He says he's leaving, which shouldn't surprise me."

"How are he and George interacting?"

Leanne shrugged. As antagonistic as always, yet George seems different around him. "I hope it continues. I'm just starting to earn George's trust and don't want anything to jeopardize that."

Tabitha frowned. "You're serious about working your way into the ranch?"

"Yes. You sound skeptical."

"Well, let's just say I don't one hundred percent trust George Walsh to follow through on his promises."

Leanne had her concerns about George, as well, but she had to believe him when he said he wanted to give her and Austin more security and give them a share of the ranch. "You know that I love working on the ranch. And for the first time in my life, I feel like I have something that's mine."

Tabitha nodded, showing her understanding. "But maybe someday someone will come into your life—"

"My husband is dead and the man I once saw as the love of my life has proven to be a major disappointment. I need to be my own boss and do what I love."

"But now that Reuben is back—"

"Stop. Now. He's only sticking around to help on the ranch, and in spite of how I feel about him, I need the help. But he'll be gone again."

"I thought he was going to do a structural assessment on the arena."

"He told me he wasn't going to, of course that was before he ended up helping us with the cows. I hope he doesn't. It would mean his working with the committee and right now I don't mind the break from him."

Then Leanne glanced at the oversize clock hanging on the wall behind her sister and gulped down the last of her coffee.

"Sorry. But I gotta go," she said. "The meeting will be starting soon and I want to get there before everyone arrives."

They said goodbye, but as Leanne drove over to the County Building, she felt as if her own thoughts were in a horrible tangle. Reuben. Austin. The past. The present. The ranch. Her future and Austin's.

Next job. Just think about the next job. The Rodeo Group meetings never went that long, thankfully, and she had to get groceries after that.

Another busy day but at least she would get a break from Reuben and the difficulties and questions he had brought into her life.

"So I'm sure you'll all be glad to know that Reuben has changed his mind about helping us, again," Reuben's cousin Cord said, glancing around the room and letting his eyes rest on Reuben. He gave him a quick grin, then turned his attention back to other members of the Rodeo Group. "So now that he's here, we want to put him to work as soon as possible."

"Sounds good to me," he replied with a forced smile. "The sooner I get done, the sooner I can leave." He had felt foolish calling Owen and telling him that he'd changed his mind. Again, as Cord so delicately put it. But he figured as long as he was sticking around for a while, he may as well get the assessment done too. Or at least as much of it as he could.

"You've barely gotten here," Owen Herne, chairman of the group put in. "Can't believe you'd want to leave so quick. This is your hometown. Lots of people want to see you. Family, old friends."

"I didn't come for a reunion. I only came to do a job." Reuben shrugged away Owen's comment even though it created a mixture of guilt and sorrow deep within him. He would have liked to connect with all his cousins and friends, but between the work on the ranch and now taking this on, he wouldn't have time. Then he caught his father's glower at his flip remark but chose to ignore that, as well. "So what I need to know from this committee is how much do you want me to do?" he continued.

"We need to know as much as we can about the arena's structural integrity," Owen was saying. "Need to know if it's worth finishing what that weasel Floyd started." Owen flicked an apologetic look Leanne's way. "Sorry."

In spite of his mixed feelings toward her, Reuben couldn't help but feel sympathy for Leanne as her cheeks flushed. It couldn't be easy to hear people put down her father. He knew firsthand how difficult life had been for Leanne and Tabitha when they first moved to Cedar Ridge. He vividly remembered Leanne's first day of school. She was quiet, soft-spoken, wearing out-of-date clothes that looked worn and tired.

But she'd had a quiet dignity and a radiant beauty that struck him immediately.

Not only him but also his brother, Dirk. Trouble was Reuben knew who and what he was. A wild child who liked pushing boundaries and testing limits. A bareback rider who prided himself on being the toughest, hardest and baddest. A rebel who couldn't win his father's love no matter what he did.

Dirk was the charming golden boy, and while Reuben had held back, feeling undeserving, Dirk, who had no such qualms, had moved in. But Reuben could never shake the idea that on a deeper level Leanne seemed to be attracted to him, as well. It had never been obvious. A look that went on too long. A smile that became serious whenever their eyes met. But in spite of feelings he'd sensed they shared, he'd also known she would never break up with Dirk.

But then she did. When she walked onto the beach at his cousin's wedding, alone, barefoot, wearing a flowing pink dress, his heart had kicked into overdrive.

And they'd spent a glorious few weeks together.

Six weeks later she and Dirk eloped. Eight weeks later his brother was dead.

"We aren't entirely sure about the integrity of the building," Owen said, pulling Reuben's thoughts back to the present. "Given that Floyd didn't finish the work, we need to start assessing the building from the ground up. We have to decide if the structure is worth working on or if we should doze it and start from scratch. What we want from your assessment is which direction we should go."

"I should be able to give you that information," Reuben said, dragging his gaze away from Leanne to the assembled members of the group who were looking at him expectantly. "It will probably take me about a week or more to cover all the aspects of the structure. Wiring, plumbing, anything that is in place. Make sure it's all up to code. I'll need to stop at the town office to see what the building permit looks like, whether we'll need a new one or if the old one is still valid."

"Could you give us an idea of what kind of money we're talking for your work?" Owen asked.

"I'll give you a discount on my usual fee," he said, keeping his comment deliberately vague. "It'll be a fair price."

"Leanne, you got that?" Owen said with a grin. "Make sure you mark down that he said a fair price. I know what kind of guy Reuben used to be. Left us hanging with the bar tab one too many times after a rodeo competition."

"Those were the old days." Reuben managed a feeble grin in response to the reference to his rodeo days. Leanne didn't need to be reminded of his former life.

"Anyone else have any questions for Reuben?"

Carmen Fisher, the manager of George's hardware store, sat back in her chair looking concerned but said nothing. Andy just shook his head. Cord was already tapping out a text on his cell phone as he got up, also shaking his head. George just shrugged.

"Okay. Then this meeting is adjourned," Owen said. "We won't need to have another one until Reuben has some information to give us."

Owen gave Reuben a broad grin then got up.

"You're coming to the ranch again tomorrow?" George asked.

Reuben shot another quick glance at Leanne, who was still tapping away on the computer, then turned to his father. "I'll be there."

George acknowledged his comment with a tight nod. "Good." Then he pulled Cord aside as they walked out of the room with Owen, lowering his voice to talk to him.

Leanne was about to leave when Carmen got up. "Leanne, can you wait a moment? You too, Reuben? I have something I need to say to you both," she said, glancing over her shoulder as if to make sure no one was in the room.

"I don't have a lot of time," Leanne said.

"This will only take a few moments." Carmen sighed, then walked over to the door, opened it, looked around then closed it.

Reuben was officially intrigued as she walked back to where Leanne sat.

"So I need to talk to you about George," she said. "I feel like a traitor, but I'm concerned about his health. I don't know if you've noticed, but he's been smoking again. Tony, the young fellow who works at the store, caught him a couple of times out back."

Reuben wondered if his return had anything to do with his father taking up a habit that he'd indulged in too often in the past.

"I haven't noticed," Leanne said, frowning as she slipped her laptop into her briefcase. "He hasn't been sneaking out of the house for a cigarette that I could tell and I'm sure he hasn't been smoking in his room."

"Well, he's been doing it at the hardware store." Carmen sighed. "And he's also been short of breath lately. I think he's under too much stress."

"So do you think he should sell the store?" Leanne asked.

Carmen shrugged. "He's not that involved in the store's operations anymore, so I can't imagine there's any stress there. He only stops in to see what's going on and check on the books. If he stays it's to chat with the customers or putz around with the inventory. He likes rearranging shelves." She gave them a wry look. "However I don't know if the store is the problem."

It seemed to Reuben that Carmen didn't want to come right out and voice what needed to be said.

"So that leaves the ranch," Reuben put in, knowing Leanne would disagree with what he was going to say. "Do you think it's the ranch that's wearing him down?"

Leanne shot him an angry look. "The ranch is what keeps him going," she returned. "It's his life."

"His or yours?" he asked, his voice quiet.

This netted him another glare, but as their eyes held, he sensed a lingering doubt. As if on some level she knew, as well. But she couldn't admit it. She dragged her gaze away, turning to Carmen.

"What do you suggest?" Leanne asked. "What do you think we should do?"

Carmen glanced from Reuben to Leanne as if unsure where and how to proceed. "I know he often grumbles about hired hands and all the work that ranch requires. I wish I had an answer, but like I said I just wanted to let you know what I've seen. I don't want to make it look like I'm going behind his back, but I felt you needed to hear my concerns."

"Thanks for caring, Carmen," Reuben said, giving her a smile. "I appreciate your letting us know."

She nodded, tucked her notebook under her arm and then left.

Leanne wasn't looking at Reuben as she slipped a sheaf of papers into her briefcase, then zipped it shut. He knew she wasn't going to address what Carmen brought up. So he would.

"So, what do you think of what Carmen told us?" he asked, pushing the issue.

Leanne swung the strap of the briefcase over her arm, her eyes looking everywhere but at him.

"Even if he isn't smoking that much, we both know he's not well," Reuben pressed. "So if there are other factors at play..."

Leanne closed her eyes, her hands clenched on the straps of the case. Then she turned to him.

"We might as well get to the heart of it. You think we should sell the ranch," she said.

Reuben lifted his shoulder in a half shrug. "I think you need to be realistic about what you and George can manage."

"You've never cared about that place at all," she continued, as if he hadn't even spoken. "You've never understood what your father has done to maintain it and keep it going without either of his sons around." Her eyes snapped as she looked at him.

"Why should I have cared or invested any more time in it? It was always going to go to Dirk, and it's not like he was that involved. You know that."

Leanne didn't respond to his assertion.

"Besides, you're wrong," he said, feeling an unreasoning desire to try to redeem himself in her eyes. "I cared more about the ranch than Dirk ever did. Worked harder on the ranch than my brother ever did. I loved my brother, you know that. But everything always came so easily to Dirk. He didn't value things as a result. He never had to work for the ranch or anything else in his whole life."

Including you, he wanted to say but he wasn't that dumb.

Leanne looked down at the table, the fingers of her one hand sliding up and down the strap. "I know that."

Her admission surprised him.

"I'm glad you're here," she said, adding to his shock. "I'm glad you're helping. George may not admit it, but I think he feels the same."

Reuben wondered if she was simply trying to make him feel good. But the lonely part of him that had always yearned for his father's approval and for Leanne's thanks was only too willing to take it all.

"Well, that's good."

"And I hope you know I appreciate the help, as well." This time she looked over at him and gave him a gentle smile.

Their eyes held, and old attractions, old emotions shimmered between them.

His breath caught in his throat and, to his dismay, he had to fight the urge to close the gap between them. To cup her face with his hand.

To kiss her.

He shook off the feeling, dragging his gaze away.

"That's good. I'll be there tomorrow," he said, fighting to regain control of himself.

She hesitated a moment as if she wanted to say more, but he kept his eyes averted.

Because he knew, if he looked at her again, he would do something supremely foolish.

Something he was sure he would regret.

Chapter Five

"So where's Austin?" Reuben asked, as he followed Leanne to the corrals.

It was late Friday morning and the sun shed weak warmth on the day, easing the chill that night had brought.

"George is bringing him to Tabitha's today. He can't take care of him and there's no way we can have him around." Leanne slipped a ball cap on her head, tugging her ponytail through the hole in the back, and zipped up the down vest she'd put on over her jacket. She hadn't wanted to admit it to herself but this morning, for the first time in weeks, she'd woken up with a sense of anticipation of the work ahead.

This morning she would have someone helping her who was competent and capable. That it was Reuben was unfortunate, but thankfully Chad would also be around as a buffer. She wasn't ready to spend an entire day alone with Reuben.

Yesterday, for just a moment, she felt as if she'd gone back in time and the old feelings she had thought she had suppressed, forgotten, had come drifting to the surface. It would be too dangerous to acknowledge them now.

"He'll probably head to the hardware store and then the Brand and Grill for coffee," she continued, "so I don't expect him back for a while. And Chad called to say that he'll be here in about twenty minutes."

"I thought Shauntelle usually took care of Austin?" Reuben said.

"She couldn't today. She's getting ready for the farmers' market tomorrow." She walked faster than Reuben, trying to keep ahead of him and the unwelcome feelings being too close to him created. She couldn't allow herself to give in to them. Reuben was leaving. He'd made that very clear.

"So he gets bounced back and forth between Tabitha and Shauntelle?"

"Why does this matter to you?" She strode over to the tack shed off the main barn and slid open the large rolling door, taking refuge in annoyance at his questions.

"Because. He's my son," he said, following

her. "I wonder if it's a good idea to pass him around like that."

Leanne spun around, her hands planted on her hips, thankful for the outrage flowing through her. "You haven't been a part of his life for almost three years and now you're going to get all parental?"

Reuben held her angry glare beat for beat, his own eyes narrowed. "Isn't that what you want? Or am I simply supposed to say, 'Okay, I acknowledge that he's my son. Here's some money—'"

"I don't want your money. I only want… I only wanted you to…" She paused there, suddenly in unfamiliar territory. She never thought she'd be confronting Reuben again. She thought his denial of Austin's paternity had put him out of their lives for good.

But he was back and, it seemed, had his own ideas about her son, correction, *their* son.

"Wanted what?" he asked, articulating her silent questions. "Me to be an involved father? Or am I just supposed to admit he's my son and walk away?"

Leanne held his narrowed gaze, suddenly unsure. Reuben admitted Austin was his. It was what she had hoped for forever, ever since she'd seen that faint line on the home pregnancy test.

Now she had a plan and a purpose. However, with Reuben, the man she had once loved so dearly facing her, it didn't seem like enough.

"I don't know," she finally admitted, stepping into the gloom of the shed, grabbing a couple of halters off their hooks on the wall and handing one to him. "I don't know what kind of father I want you to be."

Reuben released a sigh as he took the halter, his gaze fixed on her. "But you know what you want now, right? From life?"

She sighed, feeling the anger draining out of her. "I want a good life for Austin. I want security for him."

"I understand. And this is the place where that will happen." He looked around the ranch yard, a faint smile teasing his lips. "I remember sitting on a beach with you and talking about having six kids, a milk cow and chickens. I don't see a cow or chickens around."

"Someday." She held his gaze, memories floating upward. "I remember your saying you could only promise me the chickens."

"Because the milk cow required pasture, which meant land."

"Which, to you, meant settling down in Cedar Ridge. And you never wanted six kids." She struggled to keep her tone light but she remembered his comment hurting her at the time.

"Told you I never saw myself as a father."

"And here you are."

"Here I am." Then he shifted his cowboy hat on his head and sighed. "We could go round and round on this, but we've got cows to move. Which horse do you want me to use?"

She accepted his segue. It was probably for the best. Right now she didn't have the energy to look too far into the future.

"Mickey," she said. "The roan mare. I'll take Spud, the palomino. When Chad comes, he can take Pinto."

"I remember Spud," he said, hooking the halter over his shoulder and taking the second one for the horse Chad would be riding when he came. "I trained that horse."

"You did well with him," Leanne said as they walked out of the darkened shed into the light. "He's a good cattle horse. Not as good as Dickens, who I was using on Wednesday. He's a better cutting horse in tight areas, but Spud is good for long hauls."

"Listen to you, rancher woman," Reuben said, a lighter tone entering his voice. "Talking all horse and cow lingo."

She couldn't help but return his smile. In

spite of their history, talking with Reuben had always come easy. He could make her smile and laugh in a way Dirk never could.

"I've picked up a few things along the way," she said. "Your dad is a good teacher."

"He can be," Reuben admitted, opening the gate to the pen. "Not so good with hired hands, though."

"No. That's true. Dirk might have been better."

"I don't know," Reuben said, walking over to Spud and stroking his neck. "Dirk wasn't very patient either. Plus he hated cows."

"You're right about that." But as soon as she spoke the words, she felt a flash of disloyalty to her late husband.

Reuben quickly got the halter on Spud, Leanne not far behind him, but as he led his horse past her, he paused, giving her a look.

"Do you miss Dirk?" he asked.

Leanne wanted to look away; his eyes seemed to be asking for more than his question intimated. And for a moment the old attraction shimmered between them.

"Sometimes" was all she dared say.

"Did you love him?"

His question was heavy with portent. She wanted to lie, to tell him something that would keep the distance between them.

But there had been enough of that, so she simply shook her head, then tugged on Mickey's halter, opened the gate and led the horse through.

"That's the last of them, I hope," Reuben said as he nudged his horse to come alongside Leanne. He'd been scouring the gullies and hollows and hadn't heard or seen any other cows. He was sure they had rounded up all the cows and calves in this pasture. Now they were gathered up and plodding at a comfortably slow pace back to the ranch.

The wind was at their backs, which made the air feel less cold. He was thankful George hadn't been around to help. Having him elsewhere gave Reuben breathing space. A bit of peace. He could simply enjoy being on a horse out in the backcountry.

With Leanne?

The hills rolled away from them, brown now, the wind holding a promise of winter. And yet he felt a contentment he hadn't felt in a long time.

"I'm glad you could come along to herd them up," Leanne said, giving him a quick smile. "George doesn't have the patience and Chad doesn't have the skill."

Reuben glanced over at Chad who was riding up ahead, keeping his horse on the side of the herd as they moved along the fence line headed toward the ranch. This was the easy part, and unless some cows decided to make a break for it, they were home free.

"I know the lay of the land so that helps. And Chad did well, all things considered." He wanted to be positive, but the reality was Chad's main contribution to the roundup was to park his horse in a gully to prevent the cows from turning that way. Reuben could see it would take a while before Chad felt comfortable on a horse, let alone become an asset to herding and cutting cows.

Once again he felt a niggle of despair. How did Leanne even think she could carry the weight of all the work this ranch created on her own?

Leanne sighed, shifting in the saddle. "I'm glad this is the last of them. We'll just have to process them and then we can put them in the winter corrals."

"That's still a lot of cows to feed over the winter."

Leanne nodded and Reuben struggled to keep his comments to himself. It didn't matter what he thought of her trying to run a ranch with George and Chad—depending on how long he lasted—right now he had a job to do, so he might as well get it done.

"Did you get enough hay put up to feed them all?" he asked. He knew when he was working on the ranch, hay production was hit or miss. In a good year they had hay to sell. In a bad year, they'd have to buy.

This elicited another sigh. "Not really. I need to phone around. We'll need at least another hundred bales to get us through the winter. I'm thankful we could keep the cows on pasture as long as we could, otherwise that number would be higher."

He heard the faint note of tension in her voice and even though it wasn't his problem, panic flickered through him.

"Have you found a supplier?"

"Not yet."

"If you don't, you might have to sell some cows."

Leanne bit her lip in frustration. "Is that your solution to everything? Sell?"

"Just being realistic. You don't have dependable help and you're looking at a lot of work if you winter all the animals you have now." He stopped himself, wondering why he was even getting involved. He would only be around long enough to help, then he was gone.

"Did you ever like being on the ranch?"

she asked, tilting her head as if challenging him. "Dirk always said you could never wait to leave, that that's why you spent so much time rodeoing."

"That's not true," he countered, nudging his horse to get closer to the cows at the back. "I loved working cattle, riding fences, training horses. I think I liked it more than Dirk ever did." He couldn't stop the defensive tone in his voice. It bothered him that she was quoting Dirk to him. Dirk, who had told him over and over again that he didn't want the ranch their father kept promising him.

She was quiet a moment, as if absorbing this information. "When Dirk and I got married, he talked about living here. Settling down."

Her calm discussion of plans she and Dirk had made when they got married dug like a hook into his heart. He and Leanne had made plans too. Though she had been angling for the two of them to live on the ranch, he knew he could never have let that happen because of his father. But he had hoped their love was strong enough that she would be willing to go with him wherever he wanted to go.

"Is that why you married him?" he asked suddenly, struck by an idea. "Because he wanted to live on the ranch and I didn't?"

She turned away from him, looking ahead, as if she couldn't face him. "I told you why I married him. I was pregnant and on my own."

The set of her jaw told him that until they resolved the issue of the mystery texts, they would always hang between them. And right at that moment, he was tired of the distance. He wanted to find a way to make things better before he left.

"It must have been difficult for you," he said. "To be in that position."

He looked ahead, his eyes on the cows as they moved along, but most of his attention was on the woman beside him.

"It was. Thanks for acknowledging that."

"Dirk was a good man," he said. "I'm glad he helped you out when…when you needed it."

"Ironic that he wouldn't marry me before. And when he finally did, we had only two weeks…" her voice trailed off and he realized that in spite of the history between them and how things had transpired, he should have guessed Leanne would be grieving the loss of the history she and his brother shared.

"I'm sorry," he said, moving his horse closer to hers. As he did, their legs touched and awareness flickered through him. Then, in spite of the voice in his head warning him not to not get too involved, to keep his distance, he reached over and put his hand on her arm, squeezing gently. "I miss him too."

To his surprise she didn't pull away, letting their shared grief connect them.

Then she turned to him. "I wish things could have been different. For us."

He held her gaze, shock and another, older emotion flowing up into his soul. Yearning.

For a moment, he wondered, the possibilities teasing him. He and Leanne and Austin. Together.

On the ranch? With George?

"I wish they could be different too," he said. Their eyes held a moment, and it was as if time wheeled back to a better place. When they were full of plans, focused on the same thing.

Not like they were now. Alone yet bound together by their son.

Then her horse turned its head, pinning one ear back, and Reuben recognized the signal Spud was giving his horse, Mickey, to keep its distance. As he moved away, reality doused any sentimental feelings he might have been harboring.

Stay focused on your plans, he reminded himself. *Leanne is a part of your past.*

And Austin?

Reuben pulled in a steadying breath. He felt as if he, Leanne and Austin were suspended in an uneasy limbo and he wasn't sure how to resolve it. He knew he couldn't give up on plans he'd spent the past four years putting together.

But could he walk away from Leanne again? Or turn his back on his son?

"So what did you think of what Carmen said. About George?" Leanne asked.

Reuben looked ahead as he shifted his thoughts to his father, swaying with the easy motion of his horse. The saddle leather creaked, the occasional lowing of the cows broke a silence he never experienced living in the city. "You've never caught him smoking?"

"No. And I'm sure he doesn't smoke in his room."

"You're in the other wing of the house," Reuben teased. "You wouldn't know if he was."

Leanne shrugged her reply.

"I have to tell you, though, that he's aged a lot since the last time I saw him," Reuben continued. "He looks tired."

"He's had a lot to deal with the past few years."

Reuben acknowledged that with a nod, but to him that didn't change the fact that his father seemed to have lost his will to keep the ranch afloat.

"You like working with my dad?" he asked.

Leanne looked away, hunching her shoulders as if in defense. "He's a...complicated man. But I also think he's lonely. Losing Dirk was hard on him." She looked over at him. "And you haven't been around much."

Reuben released a harsh laugh. "I doubt he's missed me," he said.

"I've never dared ask him, but maybe you can tell me, why is he still so upset with you?"

He paused, weighing his answer, trying to figure out how he was supposed to encapsulate all those years of stress and fighting and disagreement into a conversation that would end as soon as they got to the corrals.

"I know that part of it had to do with your mother," Leanne ventured.

"She was one reason. Dirk was the son of the loving mother and doting wife. I was the son of the woman who made George look like a fool. I was a reminder of the woman who left him."

"Could part of his treatment of you have been your behavior? You were quite the rebel."

"A rebel you were trying to avoid."

"Yes. I was, but it was hard at times."

Her admission surprised him, as did the flush that heightened the pink of her cheeks. His thoughts drifted back to those two weeks when they could finally admit to the feelings that had always hovered.

"What made you change your mind? When we were in Costa Rica? What made you think I was worth spending time with then, besides having broken up with Dirk?"

"I always thought you were worth spending time with, Reuben. And that was my struggle."

It took him a few moments to realize what she was saying. They had talked endlessly when they were together in Costa Rica. About how they had always cared for each other. How she had clung to her relationship with Dirk longer than she should have. When he found out she'd married Dirk, however, he had wondered if it was the exotic location and the distance that had made them both so candid about the feelings they both had kept to themselves for so long.

Now, here on the ranch, where life had always been complicated for both of them, she was saying the same thing she had then.

He took a chance and once again moved his horse closer, sensing a breaking down of the walls she had put up the moment she first saw him. "It was my struggle too," he said. "Watching you with Dirk when I felt that he was all wrong for you."

"Maybe he was." Leanne gave him a knowing look. "But I sometimes felt the same about you."

He held her gaze. "I knew I wasn't the best person for you either. Which was why I kept my distance."

"You didn't keep your distance at prom," she teased again.

"I couldn't help myself. Gave in to impulses I had always held back." He allowed himself a teasing smile, pleased to see her return it. "And you didn't exactly resist."

"I didn't want to then."

"And now?" The question popped out but he wasn't sad he asked it.

She turned her eyes forward, looking at the cows plodding ahead of them, her gloved hands clenched on her reins. "We have a child together. That changes a lot of things."

Which didn't tell him much. "We've had a child together for almost three years. Something you knew all along and something I just found out about."

She said nothing, her lips thinning. He knew she didn't agree and it annoyed him that she didn't believe him.

"Sooner or later we have to figure this out," Reuben said. "And I prefer it to be sooner."

"What's to figure out?"

"We've never compared stories. I think it might help to talk it through. Let me tell you my side and I'll listen to yours. They don't jibe and it bothers me that all these years you've thought so badly of me. I'd like you to give me a chance to tell you my experience."

She sighed, then nodded. "How about tomorrow night?" she said. "When we're done processing these cows."

"Tomorrow night it is," he said.

Then a calf broke away from the herd, heading off into a side gully and he nudged his horse in the flanks to deal with it. A couple of others tried to follow its lead, which kept him and his horse busy for a while. Once he got it all sorted, he and Leanne were on opposite sides of the herd and the open gates of the home pasture lay ahead.

He glanced at her over the shifting and moving bodies of the cows between them, surprised to see her watching him. Did he imagine the look of sorrow on her face? He gave her a questioning look, but then she looked away and the moment was gone.

He turned his attention back to the cows now flowing through the open gate ahead.

He hoped whatever they hashed out tomorrow would clear up the misunderstanding over her pregnancy once and for all. They couldn't resolve anything between them until they pieced together what she saw as his refusal to take responsibility.

And then? If they managed to figure out what happened, what would change between them?

Because no matter what, two things were very clear.

Leanne didn't want to leave this place.

And he would never stay.

Chapter Six

"You have a funny face, Uncle Wooben." Austin ran his hands over Reuben's chin, his soft, chubby fingers rasping over his whiskers.

"It's a prickly face, isn't it?" Reuben said, grinning down at the little boy.

He hadn't had a chance to shave or clean up after he and Leanne were done working with the cows. He felt grubby and dusty, and yet it felt so good to have his son sitting on his lap.

"I wike you here for supper," Austin said, returning Reuben's smile.

"I *wike* me here for supper too," he repeated, avoiding Leanne's slightly guilty look.

Yesterday, after bringing the cows in, he'd gone with her to the house to spend some time with Austin. But by the time Shauntelle dropped him off, the little guy was tired and out of sorts, so Reuben had only had about ten minutes with him before Leanne decided he needed a bath.

It had been a slightly awkward moment. George had escaped to his bedroom, which left Reuben alone in the kitchen unsure of his status or what was expected. So he left too.

But Leanne had promised they would talk tonight. So this afternoon, when they were done with the cows, he walked directly to the house with her. George had brought Austin home and he'd also brought pizza. Reuben stayed and helped set the table for four and sat down beside Austin as if he belonged there.

"And you have a dirty face," he said, rubbing away a smear of tomato sauce from the pizza he had gobbled down.

Austin just grinned, and as Reuben looked into the little boy's face, he was surprised at the sudden surge of protectiveness he felt. His boy. His son.

"I wuv pizza," he said, nestling into Reuben, tucking his head under Reuben's chin.

He held the boy close, enjoying the feel of him in his arms and at the same time fighting down a glimmer of anger that Leanne had kept this from him.

He caught her looking at them but he couldn't decipher her expression. It seemed as if she wasn't sure what to think of Austin sitting on Reuben's lap.

He struggled to sort out his own confused emotions. Where were he and Leanne supposed to go now? How were they supposed to deal with this little boy in a way that was best for him?

Could he truly be a father for him?

He pushed the troubling questions aside. Right now, the next thing in front of him was sitting down with Leanne and sorting out the confusion of the past.

Then Austin yawned and Leanne got up. "I think it's time to put the munchkin to bed," she said, walking around the table.

She went to take Austin from Reuben but the little boy burrowed deeper into his arms. "No. Stay with Uncle Wooben," he cried.

Reuben had to admit, it did feel good to have Austin reluctant to leave him.

"You'll see Uncle Reuben again."

"See you tomorrow?" Austin asked Reuben, leaning back and grabbing his face between his hands.

Tomorrow was Sunday, which meant church. Reuben held the boy's trusting eyes and then nodded. He could do church. For his son's sake.

This seemed to satisfy him, so he crawled

off Reuben's lap, took Leanne's hand and followed her out of the kitchen.

This left George and Reuben alone for the first time since he had come here.

"Thanks for having me over for dinner," Reuben said in the quiet following Leanne's departure.

"It was just pizza" was his father's gruff response. "And it was Leanne's idea."

As he had on Friday, George had stayed in town, supposedly working at the hardware store. Leanne had been frustrated with his absence, but George's being gone made things easier for Reuben. The work had gone smoothly and had been surprisingly peaceful. Chad seemed to be catching on and they got finished early.

Reuben was glad. He had checked the forecast and Sunday afternoon it was supposed to start snowing.

"Eating pizza here is a lot nicer than sitting by myself at the Brand and Grill listening to Sepp berate the newest waitress," Reuben said as he got up to clear the table.

"Sepp should never have let Tabitha go," George said in another rare moment of supporting a Rennie.

"She and Morgan sure seem happy." Reuben closed the boxes of pizza and stacked their plates.

"Yeah, but it won't be easy for them once they get married. Especially if Tabitha has to raise Morgan's kid. Sometimes you're better off staying single than putting yourself in that mess."

Reuben's hands slowed as what his father said set in. "What are you trying to say?" he asked.

George glanced past him, listening, but all they could hear was the muted sound of Leanne talking to Austin.

George turned back to Reuben. "You know, I didn't like the idea of Leanne helping out on the ranch, but she's a hard worker. And she loves the ranch. I want to make a place for her here. You need to know, most of the ranch and the store will go to Austin, but I want to give her something of her own. Because of Dirk. You're leaving soon for some job that sends you all over the place." George's eyes narrowed as he leaned forward. "I know you don't like it here. You're leaving and Leanne wants to stay. I want you to keep your distance. You can't give Leanne and Austin what they need."

Reuben held his father's gaze; the old familiar and unwelcome hurt spiraling up and clenching his soul. He wished he could let it slide off his back, but he was feeling defenseless and vulnerable. Spending the last few days with Leanne, then tonight, sitting at the supper table with Austin, his son, in a house where he'd never felt at home. All this had created a confusion he was tired of battling.

He had spent most of his adult life trying to prove to himself that he was worthy. All it took was a few words from his father to bring him back down.

He wanted nothing more than to tell George that the little boy he doted on so much was his. Not his beloved Dirk's. But he wanted to respect Leanne's wishes so, much as holding back the words almost choked him, he kept silent about that. But he couldn't leave the rest alone.

"Why do you think I'm such a bad person?" he asked. "What have I ever done to deserve such dislike?"

The questions jumped out before he could stop them, and anger followed the hurt his father could cause so easily. Anger that he let his father get to him. Again.

"You were always a hard kid. Always pushing, always trouble," George grumbled. "I gave you a home. A name and a place," his father shot back. "I gave you more than I should've. More than anyone else would have, and you tossed it aside."

"Was taking care of me such a burden? I'm your son," Reuben said.

George held his gaze and a flicker of something crossed his face. Remorse? Sorrow?

Or was Reuben simply projecting his own feelings onto the man who'd had such an influence on his life?

"I don't want to talk anymore," George mumbled, avoiding Reuben's gaze.

He got up and faltered, his hand grabbing for the back of his chair. Reuben was beside his father in an instant, catching him. He held him, surprised at his own response as he looked down at his father's stooped shoulders. His thinning hair. In that moment he saw his father's vulnerability.

George was getting old, and neither he nor his father had anyone else besides Austin and Leanne.

He doesn't deserve them.

Do you?

The question wormed its way into Reuben's own doubts and insecurities.

"I want to go to my room," George said, but to Reuben's surprise, he didn't push him away. He leaned on Reuben's arm as they made their way down the hall to the flight of stairs leading to his wing of the house.

They walked a few steps and Reuben couldn't stand it anymore. "You know, Dad, all I ever wanted was to be your son."

George said nothing, but when they got to the stairs, he grabbed hold of the large, ornately carved newel post and turned to him. His eyes were softer and Reuben wondered if he imagined the regret in them. Then George patted his hand and Reuben felt himself return to the young boy he once was who only ever craved his father's love.

"You were never like Dirk, that's for sure" was all he said.

Reuben's back stiffened and he pulled away as his father grabbed the banister and made his slow, steady way up the stairs.

He turned away and the first thing that came to his lips was a prayer to his heavenly father. *Help me, Lord, to know that you are my faithful Father*, he prayed as he walked back to the dining room. *Help me get through this with my soul intact.*

He returned to the dining room and finished cleaning up. As he turned the dishwasher on, Leanne entered the kitchen. Her hair was burnished like old copper by the light, and his empty heart was drawn to her once again.

And help me to get through this with my heart intact.

The prayer was one of self-defense. He knew that their son now inextricably linked him and Leanne. Yet many questions and mysteries were woven into their lives now, and he didn't know if they could draw them out without doing damage.

He knew he couldn't stay here with his father but Leanne was determined to make a life here.

And in spite of all of that, his foolish and hopeful heart still beat faster when she came closer.

"George gone?" she asked, looking past him.

"He isn't feeling well and went to bed early." He washed his hands and dried them on a towel hanging from the stove handle. "Is Austin in bed?"

"Yeah. He fell asleep right away."

He wanted to go up and see him, but right now the conversation Leanne had promised was hovering and he wanted that done.

"Did you want a cup of coffee?" she asked.

"Sounds good to me," he said, folding up the pizza boxes. He brought them to the recycling bin sitting on the deck outside. He pushed them in and looked out at the large fat flakes of snow silently falling onto the bare ground, thankful they had waited until now to fall. If this kept up, by morning everything would be covered, blanketed and softened.

He came back into the house, shivering in the warmth. “Good thing we got everything done today with the cows,” he said as he came into the kitchen. “It’s starting to snow out there.”

Leanne was pouring coffee into mugs and looked up. “I guess it was bound to come. Thanks again for all your help. Couldn’t have done it without you.”

“I was glad to help. I enjoyed it.”

“You did?” she asked as if fishing.

“I did,” he admitted. “Even brought back some good memories.”

“Really?” She shot him a disbelieving look.

“Really. Life with George wasn’t all yelling and screaming. And no matter what Dirk told you, I always liked rounding up the cows. Working on my own in the back of the beyond, me and my horse.” He gave her a grin and followed her as she went into a small sitting area right off the kitchen and other good memories came to mind. His mother sitting there, reading a book, opening her arm to him, inviting him to curl up beside her.

"You're smiling," she said. "What are you thinking about?"

"Just pulling out another good memory of my mom. Wishing I could have seen her one more time before she died and wondering if my mother truly was the horrible person my dad has made her out to be." Reuben looked at the chair opposite, then at Leanne who had dropped onto the couch. The smart move would be to sit on the chair across from her, but right now he was tired of being smart. He wanted to be close to her.

Leanne cradled her mug, watching him through the steam. "George does tend to hold a grudge, but he seems to have forgiven me for being a Rennie."

"I'm sure having Austin helped."

"He does love that kid."

"So when do we tell him the truth? I want him to know before I leave."

She gave him an anguished look. "Can you give me a few more days?"

"Doubts again?" Her hesitancy to tell George that he was Austin's father bothered him more than he wanted to acknowledge. Leanne choosing Dirk over him again. Putting her promise to Dirk over his own feelings.

"No. I just need to sort things out in my head," she said.

"Like our supposed text messages." Reuben leaned back and shoved his hand through his hair, forcing the conversation back to this difficult topic. "So tell me your side of all of this. From the beginning."

"From when we were intimate? And we agreed, the next day, that we had rushed into things too soon?" Leanne's questions held an edge of melancholy.

"We probably had," Reuben said. "But I think we both felt like we could finally be together without Dirk or anything else between us." He and Leanne had been so happy then. They had talked and talked and kissed and shared stories and secrets.

"Afterward, I often wondered if it was the atmosphere that led to what happened between us. That sense of being where no one was watching or judging," Leanne said.

"Maybe. But I also think we both knew we were meant for each other. Part of me is sorry about how things happened, but at the same time…" His voice faded away as he thought of his son, the result of that evening.

"Most people would say it was a mistake, but I don't want to think of Austin that way," Leanne said.

Reuben was quiet, not sure what to say.

She gave him a gentle smile and he was dismayed at how quickly his heart reacted. He was so easily falling back into his old patterns and behaviors around her.

"At any rate, in spite of what happened, at that time, I wasn't ready to quit on us," Leanne said. She looked away from him as if sorting her thoughts. "I wanted us to be together."

Her words rested in his worn-out, hungry soul and he wanted nothing more than to curl his hand around her shoulder, pull her close.

"I did too." The words came out before he could stop them.

She gave him a weary look. "Being with you was so much easier than being with Dirk ever was."

Her words wore away his resistance to her. He knew he couldn't give in, but he was sorely tempted as their eyes held and old feelings rose up between them.

"So why did you stay with him so long?" he said, dragging his gaze away from her.

Leanne clutched her mug. "He was safe. You were riskier with your rodeoing and running around."

"I know I wasn't the kind of guy any mom or dad would approve of."

"My dad wasn't exactly the kind of guy moms and dads would approve of either." Leanne released a short laugh but it held no humor. "And that's why I stayed with Dirk. Though I had to fight my feelings for you, my brain told me that Dirk was the wiser choice. That he would give me the security I so badly wanted and never had growing up."

"You never talked about your father," he said. He had asked, tried to find out what her life was like but she always brushed his comments off with a laugh.

Leanne took a sip of her coffee as if considering what to tell him.

"I feel like you've kept that part of your life separate from me," he pressed.

"I kept it separate from Dirk too."

"So what was Floyd Rennie like?" he asked, hoping that by finding out more about her father, he'd find out more about her.

Leanne kept silent, looking away as if going back in time to a place she didn't want to go again. "After our mother died, he fell into such a deep funk. Moved around as if trying to erase the pain. Always, he promised us the next place would be better but it never was. Often Tabitha and I were on our own, scrounging for food. Trying to make the best of what we had. We went to school hungry many times."

He had heard bits and pieces of her story, but this was the first he knew of how difficult it had been for her. "I'm sorry," he said. "I didn't know you were ashamed of your life."

"Beyond ashamed," Leanne admitted. "It was hard not knowing, for so many years, if my dad would have work or even come home at night. It's a huge thing for two young girls to be worrying about where their next meal will come from, how we were going to get the money for clothes, let alone school supplies. We moved so much and each move cost us. Trouble was, Tabitha and I ended up paying the price more than our father ever did."

"I never knew it was that hard for you. I wish I had."

She shrugged away his concern. "I think my dad was dealing with the grief of losing our mother in his own way. We were grieving too but he didn't seem to acknowledge that. Anyhow, he finally seemed to snap out of it. Then we moved here and Tabitha and I thought this was our forever home. He settled down. Got work, but then, after a few years, he talked about moving on again. So when I met Dirk, I knew I had found someone who promised security in all the ways my father never had."

"So Dirk was your safety net."

Leanne gave him an apologetic look. "Even though I was attracted to you, some of the choices you made, the life you led, reminded me too much of my father."

Regret spiraled through him at her statement. "That bothers me because I know it to be true," he said. "If I'd been a better person, if I'd tried a little harder to be the person my father wanted me to be, maybe I'd have been the guy you needed me to be."

"I don't know." She set her mug on the low table in front of them, then sat back, resting her chin on her knees, twisting her head as if to study him further. "I think you had to find your own way through life. I know it wasn't easy being the odd son out. I know, from Dirk and from my own observation, how you and George got along. And it can't have been easy to see such obvious favoritism between you and Dirk."

"I always felt like I should dislike Dirk for that, but he was a good brother to me." Then he gave her a wry glance. "Except when it came to you. He was adamant I stay away from you. Especially when he heard I had asked you to prom."

"And then you didn't take me, yet you stole a kiss anyway."

"Like I said, Dirk had warned me away from you even though, as you said, he had broken up with you."

Leanne held his eyes. It didn't take much to conjure up the picture of her in that pink, gauzy prom dress. How her hair hung like a burnished cloud around her face. He'd had too much to drink, as usual, which made him bold and reckless. They'd been standing together outside and it had been a cool evening. She'd been shivering and he put his arm around her. She hadn't resisted and when he'd turned his head to find her face so close to his, kissing her felt so natural.

And with that one, simple act, he knew he could never simply be a bystander again.

But she'd stepped back, her eyes wide with shock. Then she spun around and ran away. Back to Dirk.

"I remember how angry he was when he found out I kissed you," Reuben said, surprised at the breathless note in his voice. "It was a surprise for me how upset he was."

"He was jealous. Maybe he knew how I felt about you."

He wanted to pull Leanne into his arms

again. But he knew they couldn't return to that innocent time.

"So let's go back to the timeline of us after Costa Rica," he said, focusing on what needed to be dealt with. "What happened when you got back home? I feel like I need to unravel this step by step."

"Well, you had your business trip to Dubai," she said. "And we decided that I needed to talk to Dirk before anything more could happen. We had agreed to give each other a couple of weeks of space. To find a way to fit each other, our relationship, into our normal lives."

"And how did that 'space' work for you?" he asked with a touch of irony in his voice. "Because it sure didn't work for me."

"I missed you. Wanted to talk to you, but I also knew I needed to talk to Dirk first. Clear that up before you and I could move on without any shadows of the past over our relationship." She was quiet a moment. "But I had my concerns about what we did so I bought a pregnancy test. As soon as I got the positive result, I phoned you but I got no answer. Then I started texting and only then did you respond."

He had thought about these texts many times now, but as convinced as she was that she sent them, he was that sure he hadn't received them. They couldn't both be wrong yet…

"Do you remember the day you sent them?" he asked.

"Yes. You had told me you would be back at your home in Montreal on the seventh of the month. I had it circled on my calendar. I didn't have your business phone number, so I thought maybe you left your personal phone at home and that was why you weren't responding."

"I did, actually. I remember being angry I forgot it because I was hoping you might call in spite of wanting your space."

She nodded. "So that's why you didn't answer. You had said you'd be home that day. So I tried again."

He dug back, struggling to reconstruct what had happened. "That was right around the time Dirk was coming back from Europe, wasn't it?"

"I think so."

"What did those texts I supposedly sent you say?"

Leanne bit her lip. Then she drew in a long breath and began. "I told you about the pregnancy. You asked if I was sure. I wrote back that I was and I asked what should I do. You didn't answer right away and then you said that this couldn't be right. You asked if this was because of Costa Rica, and I wrote back and said yes. Then you said…" Her voice broke, and Reuben struggled with his own feelings as she recited a conversation he had absolutely no recollection of. "You said that you weren't ready to be a father. That you didn't want to have any part of this. I wrote something back. I can't remember what, and then I read that you didn't think it was right for us to be together. That you weren't going to acknowledge this kid. And again that you didn't want to be a father. And then you told me to leave you alone. That you hadn't signed up for this and that you never wanted to see me again." She stopped, pressing her finger to her lips.

He felt his own anger rise as he heard her recitation of the conversation. He knew he hadn't participated in that and couldn't imagine what it had been like for her to be on the receiving end of it.

He had to fight his desire to refute everything she said. And he struggled between wanting to pull her into his arms and wanting to tell her that it wasn't true, but he kept his emotions in check. They needed to get to the bottom of this first.

"What time did you send those texts?" he asked, lowering his voice, keeping his tone gentle.

"I think it was five o'clock in the evening. I had just gotten off work and thought you might be back."

He nodded, slowly piecing her memories with his. "That would have been about seven o'clock my time. Half an hour before I got back to my place from the airport. I remember because an accident had snarled traffic. I had hoped to get back in time to watch the Jays game on TV, but I was running late and I knew I would miss the opening pitch. I was ticked about that." He gave her a shamefaced look. "Sorry. Sports fan. I really wanted to call you when I came back, but that whole 'space' thing you wanted prevented me. Then, when I got to my apartment, Dirk was already there. He had a key from the last time he'd stayed so he let himself in. He had said he might stop by on his way back from Europe but hadn't made any definite plans. I felt gross and wanted to clean up, so I told him we could go out for dinner after and catch up. So if you sent them at five, I wouldn't have been home."

He frowned as he thought back to that day. Then something teased his memory. Reuben turned to her and grabbed her hands. "Dirk was sitting on the couch reading the paper when I came into the apartment. He was acting all strange. Like he was upset. I remember wondering why. We hadn't seen each other for weeks and he didn't seem excited to see me."

Leanne stared at him, her eyes wide as if she was getting to the same place he was.

"I know he didn't stick around long after I got back," he continued. "When I got out of the shower, he had his coat on and said that he had changed his mind about staying with me. He was heading home to Cedar Ridge. He said that he missed you and needed to talk to you, which I thought was strange given that you had broken up with him. I didn't dare say anything to him, so we said goodbye and he left. I was confused by his strange behavior but also relieved that I wouldn't have to explain to him what had happened between us." He gave her a look. "Instead that fell on you."

"He came to my place early the next morning," Leanne continued. "He seemed agitated and I thought it was because he missed me, like you said. And I was feeling so distraught after I got your texts."

"So the day after you get these horrible texts, he comes over to talk to you and asks you to marry him even though you broke up with him. Didn't that seem odd to you?"

She furrowed her brow in confusion, as if trying to understand where he was going.

"You said you sent the texts at 5:00 p.m. here," he continued, things slowly coming together for him. "That's 7:00 p.m. Montreal time. I wasn't back until after that. After Dirk left, I went looking for my phone, to let you know what was going on. I was thinking I might text you to let you know Dirk was heading home but all our conversations on the message app had disappeared. I remember thinking it odd at the time and wondering if I had somehow done that by mistake."

She shot him a confused look. "You weren't picking up your phone when I called the first time."

"Because my phone was still in the apartment and I wasn't. So if you sent those texts right after you tried to call again, it couldn't have been me who replied to them."

Leanne closed her eyes, shaking her head as if processing the information.

Reuben moved closer, daring to touch her as things finally fell into place.

"I know what happened," he said, fighting down his anger as he realized his conclusion fit with everything Leanne had said and his own memories of that evening. "I couldn't have been the one who responded to your texts. But Dirk could have."

Leanne stared at him, her mind whirling as she tried to make sense of what he said.

"You think Dirk sent the texts?"

"I can't picture another scenario. I wasn't in the apartment when you said you called or sent them but Dirk probably was."

Leanne looked away, feeling confusion at his replies.

"Why would he—"

"I think, deep down, he always knew how I felt about you. How important you were to me. Dirk was a great guy, but he wasn't accustomed to being second best. He'd always been Dad's favorite, he seemed to think everyone else felt the same about him. Can you imagine how he felt when he discovered you were probably pregnant with my son? Me? Mr. Second Best was your first choice?"

She looked at him then, too easily recalling the anger and fury and sorrow she'd felt at what she'd thought was Reuben's rejection of her.

"I think I always knew that about him," she said. Reality battled with the false illusions she'd created around both Dirk and Reuben, and a curious sorrow grabbed her heart. She had been wrong about both of them. And as she pieced together what happened, added it to her innate knowledge of Reuben and Dirk, she knew it was the only scenario that made sense.

And as it did, relief flowed through her. Relief and a realization that Reuben truly was the man she thought he was.

But behind that came a deep hurt.

"What has Dirk done to us?" she asked, her voice tight with anger.

Reuben moved closer, resting his hand on her shoulder.

"He played on your fears. And mine."

"What fears did you have?"

"That I would lose you after all. That I would come so close to complete happiness and have it taken away. Again." He reached up with his other hand and stroked a strand of hair away from her face, another small connection that wore away the restraints she had placed around her heart.

She looked into his eyes, and when she saw the raw pain there, all the desolation she had felt the past three years, all the misery and loneliness, rose up. And she realized he had been hurting too.

She released a sob, then another.

And suddenly she was in his arms, her head on his shoulder, her tears flowing. She held on to her anchor in this storm of sorrow and regret and missed opportunities.

"It's okay," he whispered, his arms now around her, holding her close. "It's okay. It's over now."

Her tears flowed awhile longer but when they subsided, she stayed where she was, feeling safe and protected.

She hardly dared believe that she was here, back in Reuben's arms. It felt so right. So good.

His arms felt like home.

Then he tipped her chin up and wiped her tears away with his finger, smiling down at her. "I'm sorry you had to deal with all of that on your own. I'm so sorry I couldn't be here for you. You have to believe that things would have turned out much differently had I known everything."

"I know that," she whispered.

He grew serious as his hand cupped her face, his eyes traveling over her features. "I missed you."

His words dove into her soul and took root. "I missed you too."

Then he lowered his head and his lips

brushed hers. Gently at first. Then he pulled her close to him.

She wove her arms around his neck, her heart singing. This was how it should be.

He was the first to pull away as he cradled her head on his shoulder and leaned back, holding her close. His chest lifted in a sigh and she placed her hand on his chest, warm under the fabric of his shirt, his heartbeat as elevated as hers.

He traced gentle circles on the back of her head with his fingers.

"So now what?" he asked.

A great weariness drifted over her. A weariness created by years of anger and confusion that she could finally release.

She drew back to look into his beloved face, to take in features that had haunted her waking thoughts and nightly dreams. "We can't go back to where we were," she said.

"I don't want to," he said. "This, here and now, is how it should have been all these years."

Regret shivered through her at how long it had taken. At all the missteps along the way to here.

"I'm sorry," she said, but he stopped her.

Then he held her gaze, his own features shifting. "So what's next?"

The thought sent a faint chill through her, thinking of the plans he had in place. Plans for a job that would take him away from here and keep him traveling. His idea that George should sell the ranch.

"Can we just enjoy being together? Here? Now?" She couldn't face those hard decisions. Not after they had finally found each other. She wanted just a few moments of her and Reuben. Together again.

"Sounds good to me." He gave her a careful smile, but she knew they were simply delaying what needed to be faced sometime.

Then he sighed. "And George? Do we tell him about Austin?"

She hesitated and he seemed to draw his answer from that.

"Okay. Let's give that a few days, as well."

She could tell he wasn't entirely happy, but she wasn't ready to see what George's reaction to the truth would be. Not so soon after she and Reuben had found each other.

"We will tell him," she promised.

"Okay. I'll leave it at that," he said. He bent over and brushed a kiss over her lips.

His response created a surprising relief. She wanted to have this uncomplicated time with Reuben for a little while longer. This moment of grace, so to speak.

"So will you be coming here tomorrow?" she asked. "After church?"

"Is this an invitation to Sunday lunch?" He grinned down at her, his fingers playing with her hair.

"Of course it is. Though Sunday lunch isn't roast and potatoes. I've scaled down considerably."

"I don't think my mom ever did roast and potatoes either," he said, with a teasing smile. "She always said it didn't make for a restful Sunday."

Leanne nestled closer in his arms, toying with a button on his shirt pocket. "You mentioned I never said much about my father, but you never talked about your mother," she said.

He shrugged, resting his head on hers. "She was a good mom in her own way. I think living on the ranch was difficult for her. Way more isolating than she thought it would be."

"She was from Calgary, wasn't she?"

"Yeah. Dad met her at the Stampede. She was working as a waitress in one of the venues. He had Dirk with him and she seemed to connect with both of them. Two months later they were married."

"That was quick."

Reuben's chest lifted in a sigh. "Too quick. My dad was struggling. He was lonely and trying to raise Dirk on his own, run the ranch and the store. So they got married and he brought her out here. She managed the first year but I think it was hard for her. I got the impression from George that she thought living on a ranch would be more glamorous than it was. Watched too many *Dallas* reruns maybe." He released a hard laugh. "And then I was born, and according to the stories in Cedar Ridge, things went from worse to worst. She was gone a lot. Then one day she just left. I was five years old."

"So what do you remember of her?"

"Bits and pieces. I remember her laughing, dancing with me in the kitchen. I remember her helping Dirk with his schoolwork. He had stronger memories of her than I did. He was older. But I also remember her crying, and her and George fighting a lot. I don't think it was a happy marriage. Which is why, I believe, he's always had a hard time with me. I was the reminder of the woman who took off on him. Humiliated him."

"It wasn't your fault," Leanne said.

"I know it wasn't. But I wasn't the easiest kid to deal with after she left. I was angry and sad and I missed her, and I don't think George knew how to handle me. Plus he had to raise two boys by himself. And he was a firm believer in 'spare the rod and spoil the child.'"

"That must have been so difficult for you. Growing up like that."

"It wasn't all bad." He shrugged and looked away as if going back to another time. "I had some good memories. Dirk and I got along great and had a lot of fun."

"But you and George?"

He sighed. "More complicated. He always seemed to hold me to a different standard, and I fought it every step of the way. He wasn't the best father."

"I guessed that from things Dirk told me," she said. "I know he always felt bad for you."

"Some of it was my own doing, I'll admit. I pushed the boundaries."

"Do you think you'll ever find a way to reconcile?" Leanne put out the question tentatively. "I know George was a difficult father, but I also have seen a caring side of him. He's so loving with Austin."

She felt a shiver of apprehension at the way his mouth tightened.

"That's because he thinks Austin is Dirk's kid. I wonder how he'll react when he finds out he's mine."

Reuben grew solemn and Leanne drew back, feeling torn. She knew he was right and that was one of the reasons she held off telling George. But in that moment she felt as if she was betraying Reuben.

Just a few days longer, she told herself. She didn't want the drama yet.

"I still can't believe I'm a father," he said finally. "I didn't think that would ever happen. Don't know if I can do a good job of it given the example I've had. The father I have."

"I think you'll be a great father," she said, clutching his shoulder and squeezing her encouragement, fighting down her own concern about his reaction. "I don't think you'll be like George."

He said nothing to that, as if pondering her words.

"I guess I'll have to figure that out. Like I said, he wasn't the best example and it wasn't until I returned to God that I realized that I had another father who loved me unconditionally. That has made my life easier. I'm secure in my faith and that's been a blessing."

"That makes me feel ashamed," she said. "I wish I could say that I'm secure in my faith, as well."

"You used to be. What changed?"

She tried to figure out how to say what she felt. "Some of that has been keeping the secret about Austin. But after Costa Rica, I felt ashamed—"

He gave her a gentle shake. "It wasn't just you. It was both of us. I know it maybe wasn't our finest moment, but I know I've confessed that and I know God has forgiven me and you."

"I thought, for a while, that you were too ashamed of it all and that's why you rejected me."

"Neither of us is perfect. I've made many mistakes but I also know that God is a loving father. I know that He forgives us if we ask."

"What about George?" she asked. "Do you think you can ever forgive him?"

Reuben's mouth grew tight and he got up, shoving his hand through his hair in a gesture of frustration. "Just a few moments ago I helped George up from the table. He wasn't feeling well. I asked him why he thought I deserved to be treated the way I was. I told him that all I ever wanted was to be his son."

Leanne heard the hurt in his voice.

"You know what he said to me?" Reuben asked.

She shook her head.

"He told me, 'You were never Dirk.' That was his answer." He released a harsh laugh.

"So I don't know if it's a matter of forgiving him or letting go of the hold he has over me."

Leanne slipped her arms around him, holding him close. "I'm sorry I brought it up," she whispered. "I shouldn't have asked."

He said nothing. Instead he kissed her again and in that kiss Leanne felt his longing and his pain.

He drew away, his expression melancholy. "Can we check on Austin before I leave?" he asked.

She nodded then followed him as they walked up the stairs, her own feet heavy.

As she walked, she prayed that she and Reuben and Austin could find their way through this new place. She also added a prayer for George.

Because she knew that once they told him the truth, he would have much to deal with. They all would.

Chapter Seven

"But Joseph said to them, 'Don't be afraid. Am I in the place of God? You intended to harm me, but God intended it for good to accomplish what is now being done, the saving of many lives.'"

Pastor Blakely paused, looking down at the Bible in front of him, as if letting the words from Genesis settle into his heart as much as the gathered congregation.

"*Forgiveness* is a word that can get tossed around too easily," he said finally. "It can be something that is easier to tell other people to do than to do ourselves. Joseph had to forgive his brothers for what they'd done and that couldn't have been easy. His life was taken away as a result of their decisions."

Reuben sat back in the pew, his arms crossed as he listened to the pastor, the text hitting too close to home. The story of Joseph had always been a favorite, though he had often sympathized with the older brothers at times. He knew what it was like to watch a son being favored so heavily by his father, the son of the wife he loved more.

He glanced at Leanne who sat beside him, her hands folded on her lap. As if sensing his attention, her eyes slid sideways, catching his. The way her lips turned up encouraged him and he took a chance and slipped his hand in hers.

She slid closer and once again he was struck with the wonder of this moment. How often had he sat beside his brother fighting down his jealousy, wishing it were him with Leanne instead of Dirk?

Now, since he and Leanne had figured out what had happened with the wayward texts, he'd felt anger and disgust at what Dirk had done. How much he had destroyed for both him and Leanne.

He closed his eyes, fighting down the anger and trying to focus on being thankful that he and Leanne were back together again, instead of fighting his feelings about his brother. But no sooner did he feel as if he were in command of himself than he thought of Austin and all the time he had lost in his son's life.

You have him now, he reminded himself. And once they talked to George, then he and Leanne could make plans for their future.

Away from Cedar Ridge and George and the ranch and all the hard memories that clung to this place.

Can you do it? Can you take all this away from your father?

The thought lingered but behind that came what George had told him yesterday.

If he was to truly be himself, whole and complete, then he had to leave this all behind. As long as he stayed close to George, his father would always determine his emotions and his sense of self-worth. He had fought too hard and too long to let his father have that hold over him again.

And Leanne? Can you take her away from this?

She couldn't keep working the ranch the way it was going. Nor could his father keep it up.

Can't you stay?

He pulled Leanne a little closer, turning his attention back to the sermon, pushing that question aside, as well. After what his father had said last night after Reuben had bared his soul, he knew he and his father could never reconcile.

"I think the biggest mistake we make in forgiving is thinking that it is an emotion," the pastor continued. "Forgiveness, like love, is often a decision. When you forgive someone, you release the power you have given them over you."

On one level Reuben knew what the pastor was saying, but he still felt hurt by his father's inability to apologize. How could Reuben forgive an unrepentant man?

He looked over at Leanne, feeling so confused. He'd thought being with her would resolve the hurt in his life, and while it had given him a tremendous sense of fulfillment, he still wasn't sure what to do about his relationship with his father. Would he ever find a place of peace with George? Would he ever feel he measured up?

And that's why you have to leave.

Half an hour later the service was over and he and Leanne were walking out. Together. The few curious glances he caught made him guess that this would be a topic of conversation over a few Sunday meals. He knew his reputation preceded him, but he didn't care what people thought.

George hadn't come to church this morning. According to Leanne, he wasn't feeling that well, so even that made him feel freer.

Leanne was holding his hand, was at his side and they were going downstairs to get their son.

He clenched Leanne's hand a little harder at that thought.

"Is everything okay?" she asked.

"Yeah. Everything is great." He flashed her a smile.

They walked down the hallway to the nursery and, as Leanne signed the paper beside her name, the attendant opened the half door and Austin came bounding out. "Uncle Wooben," he called, his arms held out.

His son's pure joy at seeing him made up for the fact that his son still thought of him as his uncle.

Baby steps, he reminded himself.

"Reuben. Good to see you here," a familiar voice called out.

Reuben turned to see his cousin Cord walking toward him. His cousin's eyes flicked from Reuben to Leanne, who now stood beside him, a question in them. But thankfully he said nothing as his gaze slipped back to Leanne. "Did you get all the cattle moved?"

"Just in time," Leanne said.

"The snow is coming down now," Cord said. "Wouldn't be surprised if we get at least six inches today and tonight."

"We'll have a white Christmas after all," Leanne said.

"Which reminds me." Cord snapped his fingers. "Dad was thinking of having a Walsh family Christmas at the ranch. He wanted to have George and Leanne and Austin come, and now that you're here, you can come too. We're going to get together with Aunt Fay Cosgrove, as well. Not sure if cousin Noah will be around—who knows with him?"

Reuben wondered if they would be here at Christmas. He hadn't been home for either Thanksgiving or Christmas for the past ten years and he hadn't figured on being around this year.

But he could see that Leanne was considering the offer.

"Let me think about it," Reuben said. "I'll let you know by next week."

"Perfect." Cord nodded at the attendant behind them, then the door opened again and a chubby toddler with blond, flyaway hair scooted out and headed past Cord. He scooped the boy up before he could make his escape and shook his head at Reuben. "Kid does this every time. It's like he won't even acknowledge his own father."

Reuben, holding Austin in his arms, felt a

moment of fatherly pride. Austin had come right to him.

"If you could let me know sooner than later," Cord continued, "Christmas is coming soon."

"I know. I've barely had a chance to get my shopping done," Leanne said. "If you have any ideas for presents for George, I would appreciate them."

"Or him?" Cord said, grinning at Reuben.

Reuben caught Leanne's blush and he felt like he was getting sucked into a whirlpool of obligations he hadn't expected.

Christmas hadn't been on his radar since he graduated college. Even the brief time that he and Leanne were together, they hadn't gotten further than figuring out how they were going to get through the next few months, let alone make concrete plans around family celebrations.

"I'm not a high-maintenance person," Reuben said, trying to find a way to end this conversation gracefully as he shifted Austin to his other hip. But no sooner had he spoken the words than he realized how it sounded. Like he was expecting Leanne to get him something, even it if was simple. "I mean, I don't expect anything for Christmas. Haven't for years now."

That made him sound rather pathetic. Time to head out before Cord asked him what he was buying for Leanne. Also something that hadn't even crossed his mind until now.

"We should go," he said to Leanne who was watching him with a faint smirk.

They navigated their way past a few more people who stopped to say hi to him and welcome him back. They also managed to avoid Tabitha, who stood with her back to them, chatting up a group of people. Leanne hadn't seen her and thankfully was already out the door. Reuben didn't want to deal with any more family plans or obligations.

Once they got outside, Austin held out his bare hands to catch the lazy flakes drifting down. "Snow. Snow," he called out, as if making friends. He wriggled in Reuben's arms. "Go down," he insisted.

"It's getting kind of deep, buddy," he said, holding Austin closer as he made his own way through the gathering drifts. "I don't want you to fall."

Leanne waited, smiling at him, her cheeks already pinking up in the cold, her face framed by the hood of her winter coat. "Isn't it beautiful?" she said, looking up at the sky, opening her mouth to catch some stray flakes. "And even more beautiful now that we have the cows all gathered up."

"Such practical enthusiasm," he teased, dropping his arm onto her shoulders, pleased at how easy it was to be with her. She grinned up at him and put her own arm around him.

"So, I hope you weren't put on the spot just now," she said.

"Well, I have to admit, I hadn't even thought about Christmas. The most important thing on my mind was getting away so I could do this."

Reuben stopped and gave her a kiss. Her lips were cool, damp from the snowflakes that had landed on them.

She pulled away, glancing over her shoulder, and Reuben felt a flicker of concern.

"Are you worried about who's watching?" he asked, trying to inject a teasing note into her voice.

She said nothing, confirming his suspicions.

"It's early for us yet," she said, pulling away from him and fussing with Austin's jacket, zipping it up, fiddling with his toque as Austin pulled away. "I'm still trying to get accustomed to the idea. We've got a lot of time to make up for."

He had to agree with that.

She gave him a conciliatory smile. "This is

all new to me yet too," she said. "I have Austin to think of and how this all looks."

"So you're concerned what people think? Dirk's former wife now dating his out-of-control brother?"

"No. Of course that's not why," she said, shooting him a frown. "You just got here a week ago and we've already sat together in church."

"Which in a town like Cedar Ridge means we should be registering at Bed Bath & Beyond."

She laughed, which eased away the tension somewhat. "According to some, yes." She tucked her arm in his as they walked through the gathering snow to his truck. He had picked her up from the ranch, wanting to spend as much time with her as he could. "I want us to be sure of where we're going. And we have to think of Austin."

"I appreciate your caution," Reuben said, "but I've waited a long time for this to happen."

She stopped, held his arm and looked up at him. "Me too," she said, cupping his face with her hand, stroking his cheek with her thumb. "Me too."

The sincerity of her expression and the yearning he saw in her eyes eased his concerns.

But afterward, as he strapped Austin into

his car seat, Reuben knew a lot needed to be resolved before he and Leanne found their happy-ever-after.

"Faster. Faster." Austin grabbed the sides of his sled, squealing his delight as Reuben, who had been pulling him around the snow-covered yard of the ranch at a more sedate pace, starting running. It was a beautiful Monday afternoon. After the heavy snowfall of yesterday, the sun was finally shining and it reflected off the snow, almost blinding Leanne. But it also created a stunning winter wonderland as the snow softened the spruce trees and laid a blanket of white on the mountains behind them.

Leanne took a photo with her phone, then simply enjoyed the sight of Austin with his father.

"You taking over anytime?" Reuben panted as he ran past her.

"Why? You're doing such a fantastic job," she called out as she snapped another photo. She looked behind her. George had come outside to watch for a few moments but headed back to the house again. Leanne knew that George was avoiding Reuben and, though it troubled her, it had also been a minor relief to spend yesterday with Reuben and Austin without George's disapproval washing over them.

After church on Sunday, he had sat with them all long enough to eat a bowl of soup and then had left for town to visit with his brother, Boyce. Today, however, he had no excuse. Shauntelle couldn't babysit, nor could Tabitha, but thankfully George had been willing to watch Austin while she and Reuben fed the cows this morning. Chad had to leave early for a dentist appointment. Reuben's work in town was done early, and he was able to help her out.

It had been fun working with Reuben. She could have managed on her own but it would have taken her much longer. It was nice to have someone cutting the strings of the bales and watching the gates while she went back for more hay. By the time they were done, it was still light enough for Reuben to take Austin out on the sleigh.

Reuben pulled Austin up to join her, chest heaving as he dropped his hands on his knees, bending over to catch his breath.

"This kid is heavier than he looks," he gasped.

"And you are a lot more out of shape than I thought," she returned. "You wouldn't last a minute in a snowball fight."

"Yeah. Says you." Reuben dropped the rope, got down and grabbed a handful of snow. He packed it together, then tossed it at her. However she saw it coming and dodged, squealing. She ducked down to make a snowball, as well, but before she could toss it at him, he hit her square in the chest with another snowball.

"Pretty quick on the draw," she teased, then lobbed hers at him.

And it hit him right in the face.

"Oh. I'm sorry," she said, covering her laugh with her mittened hand, taking a step back as the snow slid down his nose, dripping onto his chin.

He stared at her and she could see by the way his eyes zeroed in on her that revenge was on his mind.

Instinct kicked in and she turned and ran. But while her red ankle boots were warm and cute, they were made for walking, not running in loose snow. A few steps was all it took for Reuben to catch up to her and grab her by the waist.

The momentum threw them both off balance. Reuben twisted and cushioned her fall.

"You're going to regret that deadly aim," Reuben said with a laugh as she pulled away. He tugged her back, grabbing a handful of snow.

"What are you going to do?" she asked, pushing her hands against his snow-covered coat.

"You'll find out."

But she didn't have a chance to because right at that moment Austin started crying. "No. No hurt Mommy," he called out, trying to get off his sled.

She struggled to her feet to comfort him but Reuben was a few steps ahead. He picked up the crying little boy. "It's okay. Mommy and Daddy were just playing."

Shock jolted though her at his unwitting use of the term *Daddy* and Reuben glanced her way, as well, as if he realized what he had said.

But Austin was pulling away from him, reaching for Leanne, sobbing now, his toque hanging over his eyes, his mittens falling off.

Leanne took him from Reuben and cuddled him close, pushing his hat back so he could see. "Don't cry, sweetie. Mommy's okay."

She looked over at Reuben, who stayed where he was, his hands on his hips, blowing his breath out in a surprised huff.

Austin's tears slowed, he sniffed a few more times and then he laid his head on Leanne's shoulder.

"I think we should take him in," she said, turning away.

He caught up to her, laying a hand on her arm as they walked. "Sorry about that. I didn't mean—"

She looked over at him, surprised at his apology. "It's fine. It's the truth."

"I wonder if George heard."

"We have to tell him sometime," he said. Reuben's hand slipped to her waist, pulling her close as he gently brushed a tear off Austin's cheek with one gloved finger. He looked so serious Leanne wondered what he was thinking.

"I know," she admitted.

She stopped, looking up at him, fighting with her need to find balance and his need to have the truth out.

"Every day I keep this to myself makes it harder for me too," she said, hoping he understood her own struggle. "You need to know I'm not ashamed of us. He knows we're spending time together. He said something about us sitting in church together on Sunday."

"Like I said, next stop Bed Bath & Beyond," he teased, as if trying to lighten the atmosphere.

"Is it?"

No sooner had the words slipped out than

she realized what she had said. How it sounded like she was pushing him.

His expression grew serious and then, in spite of Austin in her arms, he bent over and kissed her.

His lips were warm and inviting, and when he drew away Leanne felt a sense of loss mixed with a feeling of utter contentment.

"I'm thinking a store that's more eclectic and local," he teased.

She relaxed a little, smiling. "I like being with you."

"And I like being with you. Even feeding cows. And you know how to run that old temperamental tractor my dad insists on keeping."

"It's the only one with bale forks on it."

"See, that's what I love about you. How many people would even know what a bale fork is?"

She laughed, then shifted Austin in her arms.

"Here, let me take him."

Thankfully Austin didn't mind going to Reuben. He even laughed when Reuben tweaked his nose. "Funny Uncle Wooben," he said.

"You like working on the ranch, don't

you?" Reuben asked as he slipped his other arm around her waist.

"I do. I love the changing of the seasons and the different jobs that come with it. I feel close to nature. Close to God."

Reuben didn't respond, and she wondered what was going through his mind.

"And Cedar Ridge?" he asked.

"It's become home. It's the first place where I've ever felt like I belonged. Of course it's the first place I've ever lived longer than two years so that helps."

"And Tabitha is here."

"Yes."

"So you never thought of moving away?" he asked as he held the door to the back entrance open.

She stepped inside, temporarily avoiding the question. She sat down on the bench just inside the door and pulled Austin's knit hat off, setting it aside as she fought down apprehension.

"I've thought about it, but I've not had a reason to." She looked up at him, wondering what his reaction would be.

But he just nodded.

She knew this conversation wasn't over, and the thought of continuing it gave her a sinking feeling.

No sooner had she removed her son's boots than Austin was hurrying down the hallway to the family room and his toys.

Leanne took her time taking her own coat off, praying for the right thing to say.

"So, what did you think of the pastor's sermon on Sunday?"

Reuben hung his coat up, then he turned to her, a smile edging his lips.

"Are you wondering if I could ever forgive my father?"

"I guess I was being rather obvious," she said, pushing her damp hair back.

"It's hard to forgive someone who has never asked for forgiveness."

He gave her a soulful smile then walked away, following Austin into the family room.

Leanne stayed behind, dismay licking at her soul.

Please, Lord, help him to see, she prayed. *Help him to lose the bitterness that grips him.*

Because she knew that until he did, he wouldn't even consider staying here.

And the thought of moving was harder than she could bear.

Chapter Eight

"Maybe a little higher?"

Reuben leaned over, the ladder creaking precariously as he reached as far as he could, the red ball dangling from his fingertips. He slipped it over the spruce branch, then quickly retreated as the ladder wobbled.

He waited where he was, however, glancing over his shoulder at Leanne, who stood below him. She stared at the tree, eyes narrowed, tapping her chin with her index finger.

"Seriously? Do you think moving it a few more centimeters will make a difference?" he teased.

"Good is the enemy of best," Leanne returned. Then she nodded her approval, and with a sigh of relief he made his way down the ladder.

"Decorating the Christmas tree is not

supposed to be a marathon," he joked as he pushed the ladder to one side. He wasn't putting it away yet. He had a suspicion he would be climbing up that ladder a few more times.

When Leanne had called yesterday and asked him to pick up a Christmas tree in town after he was done working at the arena, he wanted to put her off. After all, Christmas wasn't for at least three weeks. And getting a tree felt like a commitment to a decision he wasn't sure of yet.

He didn't know where he would spend Christmas or how it would affect him and Leanne. He had tried not to feel pressured, but it was also unfair to put everything on hold while he and Leanne worked their way through this new situation. So he'd picked up the tree.

"I'm having fun," Leanne said with a wink. She turned to Austin who was running back and forth waving a branch they had cut off the tree.

Christmas music played softly in the background creating a festive atmosphere.

"That's a nice tree you bought there," George said. "Though we could have gotten a free one from the upper pasture."

"Snow's too deep to go wandering up there now," Reuben said, quashing his usual annoyance with his father's criticism, trying to focus on the rare compliment his father had given.

In fact, Reuben was surprised George had even deigned to join them this evening. Monday after his and Leanne's snowball fight, George had driven to town again. Yesterday he went directly up to his room. This evening, however, he must have gotten caught up in the spirit of the moment since he'd joined them in the family room, offering decorating advice from his recliner.

"Grampa, me got a tree," Austin crowed, waving the branch at George.

"You call that a tree, boy?" George said with a laugh, leaning forward and holding his hand out to Austin. "Don't go into the logging business, I think." The little boy climbed easily up on George's lap, looking content as his grandfather slipped his arms around him, holding him close.

The sight stoked a flicker of jealousy in Reuben. Had George ever held him so lovingly? Stroked his hair with a gentle smile on his face?

Austin quickly wiggled off George's lap and, ignoring his grandfather's protest, ran directly to Reuben, his arms wide.

"Do you like my tree, Uncle Wooben?"

Austin asked, almost blinding him as he waved the branch around.

"I like your branch a lot," Reuben said, tickling him under his chin. Austin tucked his head in, giggling. Then he looked up at Reuben, his eyes wide.

"You buy me a Christmas pwesent?"

"Austin, that's rather rude," Leanne reprimanded.

"Of course I'll buy you a present," he said to Austin. "What do you want?"

"Horsies. Lots of horsies."

"Real horses?"

Austin giggled. "No. Grandpa got me a weal horse. I want horsies for my farm."

"Well, that makes it easier."

But even as he made his plans with Austin, he felt the pressure of the upcoming season. While he was still in town working at the arena, he'd gotten a call from Marshall, his future boss, asking if he was still coming to Los Angeles in a couple of days. Reuben had said yes. While his time in Cedar Ridge had been a turning point for him, he still found himself eager to move on. More now that he and Leanne had found each other again.

He wanted a fresh start with her in a new place away from all the memories and unmet expectations. He wasn't sure how it would all play out, however.

"So I'm thinking we can hang this gold ball up by the red one you just put up," Leanne said, holding up another large ornament.

"I don't think Reuben should—"

"I'm not going up—"

He and George spoke at the same time.

"Looks like that's unanimous," Leanne said with a laugh. George and Reuben laughed, as well, creating a small moment of levity.

"We Walsh men have to stick together," Reuben added, grinning at George.

His father nodded, leaning back, a curious expression on his face.

"I think we should call it an evening," Reuben said, standing back to examine the tree.

The lights twinkled brightly, reflecting off the large gold and red balls, glittery snowflakes and gold ribbon woven through the branches.

"We're missing a couple of ornaments, though," George said, getting up off his chair. He picked up an old, worn shoebox that lay to one side and set it on the low table in front of the couch. "Austin, can you help me put these on the tree?" he asked. Then he looked up at Leanne. "If that's okay with you?"

"Of course. It's fine with me."

"We didn't put these on last year. Was a bit too soon after Dirk," George explained. "I kept the box back when you went looking but I think we can put them on now."

Curious, Reuben walked closer. Surprise flickered though him when he saw what lay nestled in the old tissue of the box.

"Your daddy made this ornament," George said to Austin, holding up a popsicle-stick sled. "And your Uncle Reuben made this one." He pulled out a wreath made of puzzle pieces spray painted green that framed a picture. "You remember this?" he asked Reuben, turning it to him.

Reuben came closer and took it from his father. A young version of himself grinned a gap-toothed smile back from the wreath frame. A much happier time. But he didn't take up the entire picture. In the background he saw a woman and looked closer.

His mother. She was laughing.

A surprising grief gripped him. He was five in the picture, which meant his mother had left shortly afterward. Why had she left him behind? Why hadn't she taken him along?

The old feelings of abandonment and loss drifted to the surface. He blamed the sudden ache in his heart on the music, songs he'd heard every Christmas he'd celebrated with Dirk and his father.

"I hang them up?" Austin asked.

Reuben nodded and handed him the ornament, pushing the unwelcome emotions back to the past. He glanced over at George just as his father's eyes met his. George's expression softened and Reuben wondered if he imagined the look of pain that drifted over his face.

What would his life have been like if his mother had stayed? If his relationship with George had been better?

Futile questions he told himself. Life moved on and he had to, as well.

He turned back to Austin to help him get the two ornaments on the Christmas tree and as he did, he made a decision. Regardless of how she felt, he and Leanne needed to tell George the truth about Austin as soon as possible. Tomorrow at the latest.

He knew they were growing more serious about each other and it was time to take the next step.

And where will that step lead? Could you stay here?

Once again the question rose up, teasing him. But then he glanced at George and all the old pain and sorrow he had dealt with as a young boy returned. The only way he could be free from George was to get away from his influence.

"Are you okay?" Leanne touched his arm, getting his attention. He realized he was still kneeling down by the tree, looking at the ornaments Austin and he had hung up. He gave himself a mental shake and stood. Then, in front of George, he kissed her.

Leanne stiffened but then she relaxed and touched his cheek lightly.

"I want this done," Reuben said, keeping his voice low but determined. "He needs to know and we need to make plans."

Leanne held his gaze, a look of fear flitting through her eyes.

"What's the matter?" he asked.

She shook her head and he thought again about what she had said a couple of days ago when he asked her about staying in Cedar Ridge or moving away.

But he needed to know. He couldn't afford to spend more emotions and energy on this relationship if he wasn't sure where it was going.

"You know we have to do this," he insisted.

She looked up at him but even though she nodded he could see the fear in her eyes. "I know" was all she said.

"What are you two plotting over there?" George's abrupt question made Leanne draw back.

Leanne glanced over at Austin who was running around the room, laughing and hopping. Then he dropped against George's knee and the man's face lit up. He pulled Austin close and hugged him tightly, flashing the smile that he always reserved for his grandson.

Dismay flitted over Leanne's face, and Reuben understood where it came from. If they told George, how would he react to the fact that Austin, the child he so dearly loved, wasn't Dirk's, but was in fact Reuben's?

"It has to happen sometime," Reuben insisted while George was distracted, tickling Austin.

"Tomorrow, okay?" Leanne turned back to him, her eyes pleading for understanding.

"Tomorrow at noon," Reuben said. "I have to work at the arena in the morning so I'll come here after lunch."

She gave him a surprised look, then nodded again.

Then, as if to stake his claim on her, he kissed her again.

Leanne returned his kiss but he could sense she was preoccupied.

He tried not to worry. Tried to let go of his concerns.

Please, Lord, he prayed. *I care for her so much. Help us to get through this. Don't make me give her up again.*

The revolving lights of the ambulance, the wail of the sirens piercing the quiet of the morning cut through Leanne's head like a knife.

She stood on the deck watching as the vehicle flew over the front yard, snow spinning from its tires, the red strobe light sweeping ominously over the snow-covered trees of the yard.

She clung to the doorway, swallowing and praying and trying to make her breath slow as she watched the ambulance's progress over the cattle guard, its lights bobbing as it made its way up the hill.

Her prayers were a tangle of petitions and fear.

Please, Lord. Watch over him. Please spare his life.

George was in that ambulance on his way to the hospital in Cedar Ridge. He'd just suffered a heart attack.

Half an hour ago Leanne had been upstairs putting Austin to bed for his morning nap when she heard a puzzling thump, then a gasp coming from the kitchen. She hurried downstairs only to see George hunched over the sink, breathing heavily.

She had rushed to his side as he complained of chest pains. The next fifteen minutes were a blur as she stayed on the phone with the ambulance dispatcher, following his instructions, struggling to do CPR as the promised ambulance made its way to the ranch.

When the paramedics came, they made quick work of stabilizing him.

And then, as quickly as they'd come, they rushed him out of the house on a gurney and into the ambulance. Thankfully Austin had slept through it all.

The cold winter air slipped through her clothes, bringing her back to reality, and Leanne returned to the house, not sure what to do next.

Call Reuben. Arrange for someone to come and watch Austin.

She needed to go to the hospital to be with George.

She picked up the phone again and punched in Reuben's number. He answered it on the third ring.

"Hey, you," he said, the tenderness in his

voice almost her undoing. "What's up? You miss me already?"

"It's George. He's had a heart attack." The words, spoken aloud sounded frightening and, for the first time since she saw her father-in-law hanging over the sink, gasping for breath, she started to cry.

"I'm coming over right away," Reuben said, sounding more alert.

"No. I want to meet you at the hospital. We should both be there." Her voice broke again and she drew in a few quick breaths to center herself.

"I don't want you to drive."

"I'll be okay. You should go to the hospital. Be there when your dad comes in. I'll meet you there once I call Tabitha. She can watch Austin for me."

Reuben protested again but she stopped him. "I don't know how serious this is, Reuben. I don't want you to miss out on seeing your father." As she spoke, the foreboding of her words dropped onto her heart like a rock.

She slowed herself down and eased the panic clenching her heart.

Be with George. Be with the paramedics and doctors. Don't take him yet.

The prayer helped her find firm ground, but even as she struggled to leave it all in God's hands, she caught herself jumping ahead and wondering what the implications would be for her, Austin and Reuben.

Don't go there. You don't know what will happen.

She pulled in another breath then hurried upstairs to change, waiting for her sister to come to watch Austin.

And as she did, another reality seeped in.

There was no way they could tell George the truth about Austin.

Not now.

Chapter Nine

"He looks okay." Reuben said the words as much to console himself as to encourage Leanne.

George lay on the bed, the tubes snaking out of him attached to beeping monitors. He looked as pale as the sheets covering his chest, his graying hair sticking out every which way. Leanne had tried to smooth it down, but it refused to be tamed.

George would be upset at how he looked, he thought. Much easier to focus on inconsequential things rather than think of how close they had come to losing his father.

The doctor had come by and told them they had caught it soon enough and that he was doing well. That he would only be in the Cardiac Care Unit overnight and then transferred to a regular hospital room tomorrow. He could, if all went well, be home by Monday.

This seemed improbable but encouraging at the same time.

"I'm glad he's sleeping." Leanne stood opposite Reuben, her hands clutching the bed rail, her gaze flicking from George to Reuben. She looked as concerned as he felt.

"He almost died." Reuben spoke quietly, still trying to understand what had happened.

"But he didn't," Leanne said. "He's going to be okay."

"For now." Reuben blew out his breath then picked up his father's hand. It was cool to the touch and hung limp between his fingers. He was still surprised at how panicked he'd felt when he got Leanne's phone call. How hard it had hit him. In spite of his feelings toward George, he was still his father.

"If he takes care of himself and does the rehab they lay out for him, it might not happen again."

Leanne's voice sounded strained. This was hard on her too, he realized. She had spent almost three years with George. Working with him, living in the same house. Watching him growing more and more attached to Austin.

His son.

"So I guess we won't be talking to George soon. About Austin," Reuben said.

Leanne released a short laugh, devoid of humor. "This definitely changes things."

As far as Reuben was concerned it didn't, but he kept that thought to himself. Austin was still his son and he still wanted to be with Leanne. Away from here.

But even as those last three words resonated through his mind, he looked down at George again. His father had never looked so vulnerable or helpless.

Somehow, at this moment, in spite of the anger and the fights and the frustration that George and he had undergone, much of that was forgotten for the moment. Looking at George looking so pale and having come so close to death had given him another perspective on it all.

"You look troubled," Leanne said, coming around the bed to stand beside him. She laid her hand on his arm; her fingers warm through the fabric of his shirt.

"I've never seen him looking this weak." Reuben covered her hand with his. He turned to her, trying to articulate his confused thoughts. "He's always been so strong. Such a dominant force."

"He's not been like that the past few years,

though," Leanne said, giving him a gentle smile. "He's definitely softened."

"Toward you and Austin."

Leanne shrugged. "Maybe, but there were times I caught him looking at old photo albums. Pictures of you, as well. I wonder if he didn't miss you too."

The part of him that had always yearned for a relationship with his father clung to her words. But the independent part of him, the one that had pulled away to protect himself, needed to reject what she was saying.

"You seem like you don't believe me," she said, her voice quiet.

"I want to, but I don't know if I dare." He paused, clinging to Leanne's hand like he was clinging to a lifeboat. "He scares me."

"Why?"

Reuben swallowed, wondering if Leanne would understand. He drew her away from George's bedside, just in case his father could hear.

He looked down at Leanne, praying she took his words the right way. "I'm afraid that I might be a father just like him."

Leanne held his eyes, her features impassive then he saw a sorrow drift over her face and she reached up and cupped his chin. "We make our own decisions in life. We're not only products of biology. I don't think you need to worry about that at all."

Threaded through her words of encouragement he caught a note of concern. As if she was worried that he was looking for an out.

"I want to be a father to Austin. A *good* father," he said, catching her hands and holding them to his chest. "It's just that I haven't had the best example."

Leanne entwined her fingers through his. "We don't parent completely on our own, you know. We live in a good community and we have our faith to guide and help us."

"There it is again," he said.

"What?"

Reuben glanced over at his father, still struggling with conflicted emotions. "That word," he said turning back to her. "*Community.* You want to stay here and nurture the roots you've put down. I feel like I need to leave and give myself a chance to be independent of…expectations. Be away from… well…my dad."

Leanne tugged on her hands to pull them away but he wouldn't release them.

"I don't want this to come between us," he said, lowering his voice, hoping she heard the urgency in his words. "We've waited a long time for this, and I want this to work. I want *us* to work." For emphasis he pressed a kiss to her lips. She lifted her arms and slid them around his neck, returning his kiss, easing away the tension that gripped him.

"I want us to work too," she said, giving him a tremulous smile. "And I want to give us the best possible chance to make that happen."

Reuben nodded as his cell phone vibrated in his pocket. He felt a flicker of guilt. The nurse had asked them to turn their phones off when they came into the room. In his haste to see his father, he had forgotten. However, he was expecting a call from Marshall.

He felt he was getting squeezed into a narrower and narrower space.

"I'm going to get a cup of coffee," he said. "Do you want anything?"

"Not vending machine coffee, that's for sure," she said with a grin.

He kissed her again, then he went out into the hallway. As he walked to the lobby, the sound of Christmas carols surrounded him. The nurses had strung lights and tinsel and hung paper bells by the nurse's station in an attempt to create a festive atmosphere.

Quite the challenge in a hospital, Reuben thought as he stepped out the sliding glass doors into the outside chill.

Flakes of snow sparkled and spiraled downward, adding to the layer they already had. Reuben took a moment to appreciate the beauty and peace of the scene. If the snow kept up, he and Leanne would have to put out more straw for bedding for the cows and weaned calves tomorrow.

He caught himself, tried to take a step back from the plans he was making. He was getting sucked into the day-to-day workings of the ranch. He knew from past experience that would only lead to disappointment and frustration. George would find a way to shut him out.

With renewed determination he pulled his phone out of his pocket and made a call.

"Hey, Marshall, how's it going?" he said trying to sound more jovial than he felt. He still had to wrap his head around the sight of his father looking so weak and helpless and what it meant for him and Leanne.

"Good. So, I just got a call from Dynac. They want to meet with you as soon as possible."

"How soon is that?"

"I've got a meet and greet set up for eight o'clock Sunday evening. Can you get here by then?"

"I'm not sure." Reuben fought down another beat of panic as events closed in. "My dad's just had a heart attack, and Saturday I have to make a final presentation to the Rodeo Group I've been working for here."

There was ominous silence on the other end of the line.

"Look, I'm sorry about your dad, but I can't shift it. This is an important meeting."

"Okay. I'll do what I can."

"No. You'll be here. That's it."

Marshall disconnected the call, and Reuben leaned his head against the wall, trying to plan. He could probably take the meeting. The doctor had said George's heart attack wasn't as serious as they'd initially thought. That he was in good shape and would recuperate. He wouldn't miss Reuben anyhow.

Twenty minutes later he had his flight booked for as late as he could possibly set it and still make the meeting.

As he walked back to the hospital room, the cold air still permeating him, his thoughts shifted to Leanne and her comment about wanting to give them the best chance to make their relationship work.

And he strongly suspected she meant staying here and not moving with him to Los Angeles.

In spite of what just happened with George, he still didn't think it was possible.

Chapter Ten

"Sit on Grampa," Austin said, trying to climb up on George's bed.

"Stay here, buddy. Grandpa is still not feeling good." Reuben caught Austin by the waist and pulled him up into his arms.

It was Friday afternoon, a little over twenty-four hours after his heart attack, and George was looking much improved over yesterday. Last night, as he and Leanne kept vigil, Reuben would not have thought that his father could be coming home in a few days. But now George's eyes looked brighter and he had more color in his face. His sister, Fay Cosgrove, had come by for a short visit, and Carmen Fisher, the manager of the hardware store, had dropped by with flowers. But for the most part they had tried to keep visitors to a minimum.

"I'm okay. He can sit beside me," George said, holding his hands out for his grandson.

Reuben wanted to protest, but Austin was reaching for George, and Reuben had spent enough time with Austin that he knew when to stand firm and when to give in. Once Austin had fixed his mind on something, it was almost impossible to persuade him to change it.

He was exactly like his father and grandfather, Reuben thought with a touch of irony.

He set Austin on the bed; watchful of the cords that snaked to the monitors George was still attached to.

"How are the cows doing?" George asked, turning to Leanne.

"Good. Chad and I put out extra bedding this morning," Leanne said, fussing with George's sheet. Austin had tugged it down. "It snowed again last night though."

"Will we have enough straw or hay?"

"We'll know in a couple of months whether we'll manage or not."

"I contacted a farmer north of Calgary," Reuben put in, surprised how annoyed he felt at being left out of the loop. "He has a couple of hundred bales of hay he can get us for January."

Leanne shot him a puzzled look and he

realized how he sounded. He was planning for the ranch past Christmas when he had been firm that he was leaving before that.

"You're talking about getting them delivered in January?" she asked, lifting her eyebrows, underlining her question.

He held her gaze, wondering how to approach this. "Chad can take care of unloading."

Leanne looked away and Reuben fought down a beat of concern. They really needed to sit and talk. Make solid plans. But how callous would it look for him to talk about moving away right after George's heart attack?

Take care of yourself, he reminded himself. *No one else will.*

Yet as he looked at his father, he was surprised how much it bothered him to see George so vulnerable.

Austin wriggled away, rubbing his eyes as he moved to Leanne's side of the bed.

"Stay here, son," George said, pulling Austin back to him. But Austin shook his head and held his hands out to Leanne.

"I think I should get him back home," Leanne was saying. "He's tired."

She looked tired too, Reuben thought.

"Did you have time to pick up those Christmas presents I got sent to the store?" George asked her.

Leanne shook her head. "I thought I could do that Saturday. We have a meeting with the Rodeo Group and Tabitha will be baby-sitting him."

"That'd be good." George glanced over at Reuben and gave him a surprising smile. "I'm glad I'll be here for Christmas after all."

Though Reuben returned his smile, the usual confusion and tension at the thought of the holiday season seized him. Once again he was torn between his future job and the possibility of a life here with his father.

Don't go there. You've been burned enough by this man. He's made you doubt everything about yourself. He's never lifted you up. He's even made you wonder if you could ever be a father.

Leanne bent awkwardly over and brushed a light kiss over George's forehead. He reached up and caught her hand, giving it a gentle squeeze. "You're a good daughter," he said, his voice quiet, clearly moved by her action.

She gave him a careful smile then walked out. Reuben followed her into the hall, where the carols from the nurse's station filled the air, creating a curious counterpoint to the moment.

But she put her hand on his arm. "Stay with

your father. I'm bringing Austin home and I might take a nap too."

She did look tired, he thought with some concern. Tired and worn. Too many things on her mind probably. He knew he was worn out from all the convoluted thinking he'd been indulging in.

"I guess I can stay for a while," he said, even though he wasn't sure he wanted to be left alone with George. "I should spend as much time with my father as I can."

His comment created a frown, underlining the shaky underpinnings of their situation.

"There's something else," he said. "I have an important meeting in Los Angeles on Sunday."

Alarm flitted over her features and she looked away. "For your job."

"Yeah. I can't get out of it."

"Of course. You should go."

She didn't sound excited about the idea and he didn't know what else to tell her.

"This is important to me," he said, keeping his voice low, his tone easy.

She looked at him, gave him a smile and then, to his surprise, she leaned in and gave him a kiss. "I know. We'll be okay here while you're gone."

"I'll be back on Monday at the latest. For George's homecoming."

"That's good." She touched his cheek then left.

Reuben watched her walk down the hall, Austin on her hip, tamping down the fear that things were starting to get out of his control.

He came back to the hospital room and sat down on the chair beside his father's bed.

"Have you finished your report?" George asked Reuben. "On the arena?"

"Yes, I have. It didn't take as long as I expected. I managed to get hold of all the subcontractors right away and most of them were still in Cedar Ridge so that helped."

"And what did you decide?"

"It's viable. Worth fixing up. Say what you want about Floyd Rennie, he used good materials."

George huffed at that, but it was as if his reaction was more automatic than heartfelt. "He was still a shyster," George said.

"I hope you don't say that in front of Leanne," Reuben said, trying to keep his tone light.

George shot him a glare. "I say what I want about that man. Leanne knows he was a crook."

"But he was still her father. I know she cared about him."

"So you think that in spite of everything he did, she would love him anyway if he was alive?"

A curious tone had entered his father's voice. Reuben sensed he wasn't talking about Leanne and Floyd Rennie anymore.

"I think blood is thicker than water," Reuben said. "I think there's always a connection between a father and his child that can never be erased."

He spoke of Leanne and her father, but also of himself and Austin. Once he'd known, beyond a doubt, that Austin was his son, the feelings he had for the little guy had grown stronger every day.

George looked away, staring at the wall, but it seemed that he wasn't looking at it. Instead Reuben sensed he was looking into the past.

What did he see? Did he remember all the fights they'd had? The times George had physically punished him? The raised voices, the clenched fists?

Or was he thinking of some of the happy times they'd shared? Working together, going fishing in the creek?

"I still miss Dirk" was all George said.

The stark sentence was like a knife in his

heart. Why did this bother him so much? Why did he spend so much time and emotion on this clearly one-sided relationship?

He couldn't be here anymore, no matter what Leanne said. He was about to stand when his father looked over at him. "But you're here now," he said, holding his gaze, his eyes intent on Reuben. "And you're all I have left."

Then George reached out to take Reuben's hand. The move was surprising. As his father squeezed, a reluctant joy suffused Reuben.

George clung to his hand, looking up at him. "I'm sorry, son."

Reuben could only stare, shock mixing with an older longing. This was the first time, ever, that he had heard those words cross his father's lips.

"You look surprised," George said.

"I guess I am," Reuben said.

George pulled his hand away and the gentleness on his expression was replaced with a downturn of his father's mouth. "Well, you should be. I don't like apologizing," he said, sounding more like the old George. He drummed his fingers on the bed, as his mouth grew tight. "I know I came close to dying, and it made me think about us and how things have been between us."

Reuben felt as if they were on the precipice of something different and unknown. He wasn't sure where George was going with this or what he would say. So he simply leaned forward, inviting his father to talk.

"I tried. You have to know that." George shifted his gaze to Reuben. "You were too much like your mother to make it easy for me. You were always a challenge."

So were you, Reuben wanted to say but again he kept quiet.

"But when your mother left, I had to take care of you. I should have done better. You were my responsibility in spite of everything."

"What do you mean, 'in spite of everything'?" Reuben blurted out.

George looked away, pulling his hand out of Reuben's. "I don't want to talk anymore." He closed his eyes and folded his hands over his stomach.

Reuben guessed the conversation was over. Yet he lingered a few moments longer. His father's confession, his moment of vulnerability, had shifted Reuben's feelings. As did the fact that he almost lost his father.

But as Reuben walked back down the hall and out of the hospital he wondered if it was enough to make him change his plans.

As his truck warmed up, he brushed off the

snow that had gathered on the windshield, his thoughts jumping between the promise of his new job in a new place and the memories of his life here. He'd been away so long, could he come back?

He got into his truck, pulling off his gloves. As he reached to turn on the heater, he caught sight of an old scar on his wrist.

I'm sorry.

Reuben put his truck into Drive, backed up and spun out of the parking lot, snow spitting out behind him.

He didn't know if it was enough.

"Are you okay?" Leanne laid her hand on Reuben's shoulder. He'd been in a dark mood ever since he'd come back from the hospital.

"It's hard…seeing my father so weak." He dragged his hands over his face as if trying to erase what he had seen.

"The doctor said he'll be okay," Leanne said, tightening her grip.

"I know." He sucked in another long breath and Leanne sensed something else was going on.

But she left it alone. She couldn't force it if he wasn't ready.

The dishes were done and Austin was already in his pajamas, ready for bed, cheeks shining from his bath. Leanne had put Christmas music on the stereo and the twinkling lights of the Christmas tree should have made her feel more content. But Reuben's mood created a sense of unease.

Then Austin scooted over, carrying a book that Leanne had bought for him this afternoon and he dropped it on Reuben's lap. "Read it," he demanded.

Reuben laughed, seemingly letting go of his previous bad mood, and pulled the little guy up on his lap, snuggling him close as he opened the book and started reading. Leanne relaxed at the sight, watching Reuben, his head bent over his son's.

Father and son.

How often had Leanne dreamed of this moment? The three of them together in the ranch house, making it a home?

Austin looked intently at the story Reuben read about a colt that had gotten lost and was trying to find its mother by talking to other farm animals. Reuben changed his voice for each of the animals as he read, making Austin laugh.

When the book was finished, Austin turned to the first page again. "Read it again," he said.

So Reuben did, but when he came to the

end again, Austin started yawning. Nevertheless, he flipped the book to the beginning. "Again," he demanded. "Read it again."

"I think someone needs to go to bed," Reuben said, closing the book.

"No. Read it. Read it. Read it." Austin's voice grew louder and shriller and Leanne saw his tears gathering as he tugged on the book.

"No, buddy. You need to go to sleep." Reuben tried to take the book from him but Austin wriggled in his arms, a small bundle of fury.

"No sleep. *Read!*" Austin yelled, his face red, tears of anger streaming down his cheeks. He swung the book around and hit Reuben on the face with the corner.

"Ouch. That hurt." Reuben caught Austin by the arms, staring down at him, eyes narrowed. Austin was suddenly quiet, as if sensing he had pushed things too far.

Then Reuben abruptly set Austin aside. He jumped up from the couch and strode into the dining room.

Austin started crying again and Leanne picked him up, wiped his eyes and then brought him upstairs.

"See Uncle Wooben," Austin whimpered

as Leanne closed the door of his room behind them.

"No. You hurt him with your book," Leanne said, keeping her voice quiet. She was still surprised at the look of horror on Reuben's face when he had reprimanded Austin.

"I sorry," Austin said, hanging his head.

"That's good. I'll tell… Uncle Reuben." She faltered over those last words, a sense of dread tightening her abdomen. They had to tell Austin. It wasn't fair to keep this from him much longer.

But that would mean telling George, and now, with him just recuperating from the heart attack, when could they do that?

She tucked Austin into his bed, and as she sang his bedtime prayers with him, the door opened and Reuben stepped into the room. He stood by the door, as if uncertain what to do but then Leanne waved him over.

He came by the bed and Austin grinned up at him, everything forgotten. "I wove you, Uncle Wooben," he said.

Reuben dropped to his knees beside the bed and pulled Austin to him in a tight hug. "Love you too," he whispered.

Reuben pulled away. Leanne hugged Austin, then kissed him good-night. Reuben left the room, Leanne behind him. She kept the door open, following Reuben down the stairs. He walked into the family room but didn't sit down. Instead he turned to her, looking anguished.

"I'm sorry I got angry with him. I shouldn't have."

"He was being a little stinker," Leanne said, touching his arm to reassure him. He looked so distraught.

"But I felt…I thought I was…" He stopped, dropping his one hand on his hip, the other clutching his forehead.

She caught his raised arm and lowered it. "You thought you were what?"

He looked at her a moment, as if trying to get his bearings. Then he pulled his sleeve up and turned his wrist around. "This scar? Remember asking me about it all those years ago?"

She traced the puckered skin, remembering that afternoon, here on this ranch. Dirk had been inside the house, watching a football game with George. She and Reuben had been sitting on the deck. Just talking. She'd noticed the scar on his wrist and had taken his hand, had touched it. It was one of those forbidden moments, and it was then that she realized that she cared for Reuben more than she'd ever cared for Dirk. It was both exhilarating and frightening. "You told me you got it when you were putting up fencing with Dirk," she said, her voice quiet. "You said you cut yourself on a nail."

Reuben looked down at it, shaking his head and rolling his sleeve down again, buttoning the cuff. "I lied to you. I got into a fight with Dad over a horse. He hit me with the bridle, and the buckle cut my wrist wide open. I bandaged it and went back to work. He never spoke of it again."

Leanne couldn't stop her gasp of shock. Her eyes flew to his, but he was looking down at his arm, his expression grim.

"Dad had a horrific temper and he would let it fly anytime he got upset. I was on the wrong end of that temper too many times."

Leanne had known Reuben had it hard but she never knew that George had been physically abusive.

"I'm so sorry. I never knew how bad it was." She laid her hand on his chest, willing him to look at her. "I'm so sorry."

"It's in the past and Dad even apologized to me this afternoon." He released a humorless laugh. "Never thought I'd hear the words *I'm sorry* come from the mighty George Walsh."

He looked at her, and to her surprise he

gave her a gentle smile, easing her hair back from her face with his hand.

"Dirk never said anything" was all Leanne could manage.

"I asked him to keep his mouth shut. It was humiliating and I didn't want anyone else to know."

"I wish I had known."

"Would it have changed anything?"

"It might have."

"I wouldn't have wanted you to date me out of pity."

"It wouldn't have been pity—"

He stopped her there. "You know, deep down, there were other more important reasons we didn't end up together. I know I wasn't the best person for you. And I know that Dirk was."

"But he had it so much easier than you," Leanne insisted. "Now that I know what you dealt with, I think I might have been more understanding of who you were."

He shrugged. "We don't need to talk about that now. That's all in the past." He stroked her cheek, looking bemused. "Don't look so sad. It wasn't all bad. We had good times too. I remember trips to go fishing up in the mountains. Long drives to go to bull sales where we played road games. George taught me how to train horses." Then he grew serious. "But at the same time, my dad had a mighty temper and I've seen him go out of control too often. And that's why…that's why…" His voice broke, creating more confusion for Leanne.

"Why what?"

He shook his head and was about to turn away when Leanne caught him by the arm, stopping him. "Please. No more secrets. Tell me."

Reuben swallowed, shaking his head. "When Austin hit me with that book, I got so mad…I was afraid I would hurt him. That's why I had to walk away. I've seen my father's temper boil over and I couldn't let that happen between me and my son. I can't let him have that kind of father."

"Of course you were angry," Leanne said, concerned at the sorrow in his voice and the anguish on his face. "He was being a brat. I was upset too."

"But you don't have my father's genetics. You don't have to worry what might happen."

"Nothing happened," she said, feeling a panicky need to encourage him. It was as if he was withdrawing from both of them. "You didn't do anything."

Reuben didn't look convinced and Leanne

sent up an anxious prayer for wisdom and for him to understand. She grabbed him by the arm and gave him a small shake. "You said you can't let him have that kind of father, but you'll never be the father your dad was. I see you with Austin. You're loving and caring and kind and patient. Way more patient than I am."

He held her gaze and she was encouraged by the smile that slipped over his lips. "You sound convincing."

"I don't need to sound convincing. You need to believe that you are your own person. And that you don't have to worry about being like your father. Two-year-olds are annoying and frustrating, and there have been times I wanted to leave him in his bedroom with the door locked all afternoon so I wouldn't have to deal with him." She gave him a reassuring smile. "That's what being a parent is all about. And I'm not worried about what type of parent you are or will be."

Reuben shook his head and then, to her surprise, pulled her into his arms. "Because of you I want to make better choices than I have in the past."

"And you have. With God's help you have made good choices. Your own choices."

He kissed her again and she settled into his arms, his heartbeat reassuring.

But even as he held her close, even as they shared this moment of closeness, she knew those choices would take him away from her. She sent up a prayer for strength, knowing that they had come to the moment she had been anticipating but also felt apprehensive about.

It was time they talked about what lay ahead and what decisions they were going to make.

But before she could speak, his cell phone buzzed and he pulled away, glancing down at the number. He gave her an apologetic smile. "Sorry. I have to take this. It's Marshall."

She nodded, pulling away, wrapping her arms around herself. Reuben walked away, sounding animated and excited.

Leanne knew this man was Reuben's future boss and they were talking about his job. In California.

She looked around the room, trying to imagine herself away from this place that she had woven so many dreams around.

Trying to imagine herself sitting alone in the middle of a large city while Reuben traveled around the world, or moving from place to place like she had with her father.

Could she do it? Was her love strong enough?

Chapter Eleven

"Is the arena worth fixing up, in your opinion?" Owen asked as Reuben put a cap on the felt pen he had used to make notes on the whiteboard in the meeting room.

Reuben looked around the gathering of the Rodeo Group and nodded.

"I believe it is," he said, gesturing to the figures he had just written out on the board. "Like I told my father, Floyd used quality materials for the work he actually did." The smile he gave Leanne gave her a surprising sense of peace. Her father wasn't such a loser after all.

Reuben sat down beside her, giving her arm a gentle squeeze. They hadn't seen each other this morning. Reuben had been busy getting his presentation together and she had been cleaning the house.

She made a few notes on her laptop, glancing at her phone as she did. No messages from her sister, who was watching Austin.

She had left her son there because she had texted Reuben last night, after he left, saying that she needed to talk to him after she visited George in the hospital. The shadow of Reuben's new job was hanging over her and she was tired of the uncertainty. Discussing their future couldn't wait any longer and she didn't want the complication of Austin's being around, distracting them.

"Well, thanks so much for all your hard work," Owen said, looking around the room at the gathering. "And thanks, everyone, for taking the time out of your Saturday afternoon to come out here."

Owen had invited members of the Chamber of Commerce to the meeting, as well, so they could be kept in the loop. The small room was stiflingly full and Leanne felt a bit light-headed. She had missed breakfast and lunch, keeping herself busy with mindless tasks. Anything to avoid thinking of the conversation she and Reuben were going to have. Part of her dreaded it. It was so much easier to float along without making a decision when, no matter what they chose, it would be difficult for one of them.

I've made so many sacrifices for men, Leanne thought, memories of her father's pleading, Dirk's constant postponing of their wedding blending with what she guessed Reuben would soon ask of her. *Can I do it again? Should I have to?*

"Thanks again, Reuben, for doing this for us," Owen said. "I think I can say for everyone here that we're happy to know that we don't have to tear down the arena. We won't be having any more meetings until the New Year, when we can ask for contract bids to finish the arena." He glanced at Leanne. "And I understand that Helen is coming back as secretary then?"

Leanne nodded, giving Owen a cautious smile. "I can't juggle working on the ranch and taking care of Austin with this job." She felt a niggle of unease as she laid out her reasons. Her decision was more complicated and would be influenced by what happened after she and Reuben talked.

Please, Lord, help me to make the right choice, she prayed. *Show me what You want us to do. Show us what You want us to do.*

"I understand," Owen said, then turned to

Reuben. "Will we be getting a formal report on this?"

"Complete with embossed folder," Reuben joked.

"Does anyone else have any questions for Reuben?"

"I wouldn't mind asking you about the possibility of adding to the building," Mr. Rodriguez said. "My daughter, Shauntelle, has spoken of starting up a snack bar and had hoped to start a restaurant there, as well. It wasn't in the original plans but she talked to an architect and can get some blueprints drawn up."

"That sounds amazing," Owen chimed in, standing up. "Why don't you come with me and Reuben to the arena right now? We can see what the possibilities would be in terms of where we could put it."

Reuben frowned at Leanne.

She gave him a reassuring smile. "I'll meet you at the hospital whenever it works for you," she said, gathering her things and standing. "Or at the back booth at Angelo's for supper."

The restaurant would give them more privacy than the Grill and Chill and it was quieter.

She slipped the laptop into her purse, and

as she stood, he laid his hand on her shoulder, giving her a gentle squeeze.

"I'll be there soon. But if I'm not at the hospital by seven, let's meet at Angelo's."

She felt a flare of disappointment but then, as he brushed her hair away from her face, she saw the scar on his wrist. Now that she knew the story behind it, her perspective had changed.

How could she expect him to even consider staying on the ranch with his father?

But how could she ever leave?

Later. Later, she told herself.

"Okay. It's a date," she said trying to inject a happy note into her voice.

He nodded then brushed a gentle kiss on her lips.

"See you there" was all she said, then she walked away, head down, avoiding the curious looks of the people gathered in the room.

"I don't want to be a burden." George was sitting up in bed, arms folded over his chest, looking determined. "The doctor said I can go home Monday so we'll have to see about getting help. I can hire a nurse to take care of me."

Leanne wanted to object but she knew it was a smart move. No matter what happened, it would be better if George had someone else taking care of him. She wouldn't have time.

"How are things going on the ranch?" he asked.

"Good in the minutes since last you asked," she teased.

He nodded, tapping his fingers on his arm. "I know. I'm sorry. I feel useless and I hate being away from the place."

"Well, no fears. The cows are doing well. This morning I talked to the guy Reuben mentioned yesterday about getting the hay hauled in and he said he could come in a week or so."

"We don't need it right away, do we? I thought we were good until January."

"No. But Reuben thought it was a good idea to get it delivered before the roads get too bad."

She saw his features tighten at the mention of Reuben's name, and her thoughts flipped back to last night. To Reuben's confession. To the scar puckering his wrist and the doubts he had expressed about being a good father.

So much of it was because of the man in front of her. A man she had come to care for in her own way.

"I'm glad Reuben has been around to help," she said. "He's done a lot."

"More than he used to," George grumbled. "Didn't always work so hard."

"He was only a kid then."

"So was his brother." George looked away then shook his head. "Too many memories I can't shed in my brain. Sitting in this hospital bed, I've had too much time to think about the past."

Leanne sensed an opening. "What have you been thinking about?"

George's lips tightened and Leanne wondered if she had gone too far. But she was tired of the unspoken words. The broken-off sentences. The things he refused to speak of.

He had pushed Reuben so hard and done so much harm to him. Reuben's revelation that he was afraid he would be a father like George was a blow Leanne still struggled with. She laid the blame for his fears square on George's shoulders.

"Dirk. I miss him," George said finally, giving her a melancholy look. "And I'm sure you miss him too."

Leanne didn't want to go there.

"And Reuben?" she asked instead.

"Well, he's here. For what that's worth."

And suddenly Leanne was tired of it.

"Why do you dislike Reuben so much?" The words spilled out of her, born of frustration and sorrow for a man she cared so much for. George glared at her and fear rose up at the sight of his widened eyes, the clenching of his jaw.

"Doesn't matter," he muttered, looking away. "It's in the past. Should stay there."

"I don't agree," she said, thinking of Reuben's expression whenever he talked about George. The fear that seemed to dog him, thinking that he could even come remotely close to being a father to Austin like George was to Reuben. If she and Reuben were to have a future, she felt she needed to deal with his past.

But by doing so, she knew she put her own future on the ranch at risk.

"Don't ask," he said in a gruff voice. "It's old history."

"What started it? Was it something he did? Because if that's the case, then maybe we can find a way to fix it."

"Can't be fixed. Ever. It's done. Finished. Over."

"Please tell me. I want to find a way to bring you two together." Even as she spoke the words, she felt a flush of guilt.

Was she thinking of her own self-interests? Did she hope that if George and Reuben reconciled, Reuben would be willing to stay around the ranch?

She pressed her fingers to her lips, a prayer for wisdom and guidance winging upward.

Help me Lord, she prayed. *Help me to say the right thing for the right reason. Help me to think only of Reuben and Austin and what's best for them.*

The words the pastor read on Sunday slipped into her mind.

You intended to harm me, but God intended it for good. Could God use everything for good? Could he find a way to make good the things that George had done to his own son?

"All his life Reuben only wanted to be your son. I know he wasn't always the best behaved but some of it…was…well…because of how you treated him."

Surprisingly George didn't respond to that.

"He was a good son and I know he loves you. All he wants is that same love in return."

George blinked and Leanne wondered if she had imagined the glint of tears in his eyes. Or maybe it was wishful thinking.

"I know."

His simple admission ignited a spark of hope. "He really cares," she pressed, sensing his softening. "All he's ever wanted was to be a part of your life and a part of this ranch."

Was she overreaching? Superimposing her own yearnings on Reuben's actions?

And yet she sensed a peace about him as they worked with the cattle, as they rode the backcountry. She knew that, whether he wanted to admit it or not, the ranch was in his blood. In his soul. "I know it's hard to believe, but he's all you have left. He and Austin are the only family you have."

George shot her a narrowed glance. Did he, on some level, know the truth about Austin?

"I think we could have a good life," she pressed, making one last case.

"I don't know if it can happen," George finally said, closing his eyes. He looked tired today. More than yesterday and Leanne wondered if he would truly be able to come home on Monday.

"You know that we have been told many times that all things are possible with God," Leanne said, her tone quiet, gentle.

"Maybe."

Leanne waited, sensing that George wasn't pushing back at her anymore. That maybe, if she could find the right questions, he would tell her why he felt the way he did about Reuben. A man who had always been so important to her and who she was coming closer and closer to love with every day she spent with him.

"I've always had a hard time with Reuben. I don't think that's any secret," George said, his eyes still closed. "I've always had a hard time...accepting him."

That was confusing.

"What do you mean, accepting him? He's your son."

George opened his eyes, staring directly ahead, his hands clutching the sheets. "No. He's not."

He spoke the words so quietly Leanne wasn't sure she'd heard him correctly.

"I don't understand."

George's mouth grew tight, and for a moment Leanne thought the conversation was over. But then he drew in a shaky breath followed by a deep sigh. "I married too soon after Dirk's mother died. But I was lonely and Dirk was so young. I was lost on my own. Reuben's mother was beautiful and fun. But my sister, Fay, warned me not to be rash. I should have listened to her. Marrying Raina was a mistake. She was hard to live with. Hated the ranch. We grew apart. We...we weren't...intimate for the last six years of our marriage." He paused, pulling in a long, slow breath.

Leanne felt as if she was teetering on the edge of a chasm, but she had started this and she had to see it to the end.

"And she left when Reuben was five."

His words, so quiet, so softly spoken, fell like rocks into Leanne's soul. Hard. Uncompromising. Devastating.

"So you're saying that Reuben—"

"Isn't my son. That's why I've had a hard time with him. He was the son of the woman who cheated on me." He seemed to spit out those last words. "And she didn't even have the grace to take her son with her when she left."

Leanne fought down her panic, understanding what he was saying on one level but still unable to process it.

"Does…does Reuben know this?"

George shook his head. "No. I was too proud to let anyone know what had happened, how Raina had cheated on me."

"But you kept him."

George glowered at her. "Of course I did. He didn't have anyone else. Where could he go? His mother died while she was on some holiday in Mexico after she left and I was all he had."

Leanne held his gaze, hearing one thing, feeling another. George cared for Reuben in his own way and yet he had seen him as an unwanted responsibility.

And as all this fell together another, horrible thought came to mind.

Didn't I do the same? By staying with Dirk so long, wasn't I also unfaithful to Reuben? I am no different than Reuben's mother.

And behind that came another revelation.

Austin wasn't George's biological grandchild. In any way.

The room spun around her as she clung to the side of George's bed. Everything had changed.

"Are you okay, Leanne?" George asked, touching her hand with his. "Your hands are like ice, honey."

Leanne closed her eyes, praying one simple prayer over and over again.

Help me, Lord.

"Leanne. Tell me." George sounded frightened and Leanne had to fight down the nausea that threatened.

Her stomach roiled.

"Leanne."

She breathed in then out then squeezed his hand, trying to gain control of the emotions that swamped her. Trying to find solid ground.

"I'm so sorry to hear about Reuben's mother" was all she could manage.

"It was a long time ago, my dear."

The affection in his voice and the way he patted her hand loosened what little bit of control she had left.

She closed her eyes as a sob worked its way up her throat.

"Leanne, what's wrong? I'm calling the nurse."

She shook her head, tears slipping past her tightly squeezed lids. "Please. Don't," she managed.

"Where's Reuben? He should be here."

"I'm meeting him. Later." Slowly she regained her equilibrium but a deep grief and shame now wrapped icy fingers around her heart.

George waited while she dug in her purse and pulled out a tissue, wiped her eyes and drew in a steadying breath.

"What's wrong? Tell me," he demanded. His voice grew louder and she knew she couldn't put him off anymore. Though she and Reuben had agreed they would be together when they told him about Austin, Leanne couldn't hold the truth back from him any longer.

"I have something important to tell you," she said, her voice quiet now. She looked down at the tissue she had folded and refolded, unable to look George in the eye. "But before I do, you need to know that I always cared for Dirk. He was someone I had thought could give me what I didn't have growing up. Security. A solid support. He was a good man. But Dirk and I were engaged for so long I never thought he would set a wedding date."

"You know I never cared for your relationship with him at that time."

"I know."

"But I did come to care for you later."

He sounded apologetic and Leanne felt even guiltier. She wasn't worthy of even that small amount of consideration.

"Dirk and I fought over it so many times," she said. "And I got tired of waiting. I told Dirk that if he couldn't choose between you and me, then I didn't want to be with him. He didn't say anything, which, to me, was his choice. So I broke up with him."

"Was that when Dirk went to Europe?"

She nodded.

"And I went to Costa Rica for the wedding Dirk and I were supposed to go to," she continued. "I already had the tickets. Seemed a shame to waste them. And, well, Reuben was there. At the wedding." She stopped there, not sure how to carry on.

"And..." George prompted.

"We spent the whole time together. And we fell in love. Even though I'd dated Dirk, part of me was always drawn to Reuben. It wasn't right of me and I know that, but Reuben made me nervous."

"He should have. He was living a careless life."

Leanne nodded. "I know. That's why I kept myself from him, but when I went to Costa Rica and saw him there, I knew I couldn't deny how I felt about him anymore. He felt the same way. While were there…we…we were together." She faltered, sucking in another breath. Sending up another prayer. Leanne kept her head down as she battled her shame. Her confession, coming on the heels of what George had told her about Reuben's mother, made her story sound tawdry and cheap.

But Austin came of that, she reminded herself. And she wasn't tarnishing the blessing he was to her. Nor was she going to deny her feelings for Reuben.

"We both agreed that it was a mistake, " she said, fighting for words past the thickness in her throat. "And then Dirk came back from Europe and he found out that I was expecting Reuben's child—"

"And he married you anyway?" His incredulity and the force of his anger sent her gaze flying to him. He was staring at her as if he didn't know her. "And after he died, you never told me the truth?"

"Dirk made me promise not to. He was so adamant about it. But the past few months I've wanted to, again and again. And then Reuben came back and I told him the truth—"

"But not me." His eyes were wide with anger, his lips white. His monitor beeped as his heart rate flew upward.

"Let me get a nurse," she said, concerned, wishing she had never told him.

George shook his head, breathing deeply.

"No. No nurse. I don't want a nurse." He took another breath and thankfully he looked more calm. Then he turned to Leanne, his eyes as hard as granite. "But you. You can leave. And never come back."

Chapter Twelve

"Can't meet you for dinner. Austin is at Tabitha's for the night."

Reuben stared at the cryptic text message he'd just gotten from Leanne, trying to figure out what to think. He had tried to call her but got no reply. So he had texted her back, asking her what was going on. Why did Austin have to stay at Tabitha's?

This was how it all began, he thought, hitting Send on his text message. Lost calls, misplaced texts. But he could see that she had read his text. And just to be on the safe side, he took a screenshot of their exchange.

Given their history, he couldn't be too careful.

He waited, watching the screen, waiting for her reply but there was nothing. He gave her a few more minutes but unless she was out of service, he didn't know why she wasn't returning his texts.

Or explaining better what she meant by "talk later."

He sat back, dragging his hand over his face, fighting down a sense of panic. He knew events had been converging the past week to a place of no return. His boss arranging for a meeting tomorrow, Leanne insisting they tell George the truth about Austin.

And, even more important, they had to make a decision about where they were going as a couple. California and the future? Cedar Ridge and his past?

The last thought created a surge of dread. He knew how attached Leanne was to the ranch and how involved she was. But he had to maintain his independence. He couldn't afford to let George take over his life and remind him of all he wasn't or couldn't be.

It doesn't have to be that way. He apologized to you. It could be the start of a new relationship.

It was an enticing idea that he had nurtured for too many years. He didn't dare indulge in it.

All his life Reuben had kept his own dream of working on the ranch tamped far down. It hurt too much to know that his father would, most likely, never accept him as a partner. In spite of that, no matter what he did, where he worked, his heart had always been here, in Cedar Ridge at the Bar W.

But now? Could it be different?

Reuben looked at his phone again, toyed with the idea of sending another text to Leanne but nixed it. If she hadn't answered by now, then something else was going on.

He shoved his phone into his pocket, fighting down an unreasoning fear that Leanne had done what his mother had. Left him.

His heart sank and his stomach roiled. No. He couldn't believe that.

Something else had happened and he needed to find out what.

He got into his truck and started driving. But his anger and disappointment with Leanne grew with each mile. Too many things going on. Too many things to deal with. Everything seemed to be converging into a situation he couldn't control.

Ten minutes later he swung around the corner of the gravel road leading to Tabitha's and his truck fishtailed, his lights arcing through the gathering dark.

He spun the steering wheel to bring the truck back onto the road, but rocked to a halt and sucked in a deep breath. Anger and driving were not a good combination.

Like father like son.

The thought chilled him to the bone. His mind slipped back to a time when he and his father had been fighting about something and George had turned to him, yelling as he lost control of the truck. When they plowed into the ditch, it had only served to make his father even more upset.

His father had a wicked temper and right now Reuben wasn't acting any differently.

He clenched the steering wheel, fighting down the fury that ripped through him. He wasn't going to be like his father.

But you are. You're his son.

The insidious voice rose up and right behind it came the memory of Austin hitting him with the book. His first response was anger, and it made him sick to his stomach that he could be mad at his son.

But what frightened him even more was that he was acting like his father.

Help me, Lord, he prayed. *Help me to make my own choices. To be my own person.*

He pulled back onto the road and at a more sedate pace, drove into Tabitha's yard. But that still didn't ease his panic.

He knocked on the door and Tabitha was right there, as if she'd been waiting for him.

"Come in," she said, stepping aside.

The mobile home wasn't large and Reuben felt as if he was filling up the space when he stepped inside the entrance, pulling his hat off his head.

"Austin is in bed already," she said.

"Kind of early, isn't it?"

"Early for bed, late for a nap." She shrugged. "Depends on how you spin it. Do you want a cup of tea?"

"I'm only staying long enough to take Austin home," Reuben said.

Tabitha's forehead creased in a light frown. "Home as in the ranch?"

Reuben blinked as he realized what he had said. "Yes. That's what I meant."

"I thought you meant the hotel you were staying at."

"That's no home."

"You're telling me. Anyhow, Leanne was quite specific that Austin stay here. She said that you were flying to Los Angeles tomorrow."

"Right," he said. "Then he may as well stay here."

"And you may as well have a cup of tea.

Not to sound all dramatic, but you look like five miles of bad road."

"I feel like ten," he said, shrugging his jacket off and hanging it over the back of a wooden chair.

"So how's your dad?" she asked as she busied herself in the tiny kitchen, boiling water, setting cups out.

"The doctor said he could come home on Monday."

"That's early."

"He's a tough old cowboy, I guess," he said, drumming his fingers on the table.

"And how is Chad working out as a hired hand?"

"He's okay."

"I know he's never worked on a ranch before. Nice that your dad was willing to give him a chance."

Why she was chatting about stuff he didn't care about? Then as she set the mugs onto the table, he realized what she was doing. "You're going to make me ask, aren't you?" he said.

"Yes. I am." Tabitha returned to the counter, poured the boiling water into the pot then brought it and the mugs to the table. "Honey or sugar in your tea?"

"Neither."

"Ah. Manly man." Tabitha brought the teapot to the table and sat down. How could she act so casual when he felt as if everything was coming crashing down on him?

"Okay. So what happened with Leanne?" Reuben finally asked.

"All she would tell me was that she had made a huge mistake and now she was paying the price." Tabitha poured some tea into the mugs and set the pot down, folding her arms as she looked over at him. "What do you suppose she's talking about?"

"I have no idea. She hasn't said anything more to me than what I told you." Reuben massaged his temples with his fingertips, as if trying to draw out what might possibly have instigated this.

"Did you two fight?" Tabitha asked.

"What? No. We were supposed to meet at Angelo's after she visited my father in the hospital. I got her text while I was waiting there." Reuben pulled the steaming mug tea close, wrapping his chilled hands around its warmth. "Did she tell you if she stopped by to see my father?"

Tabitha shrugged. "She just called, asking me to watch Austin and saying that she needed some space."

That word again. That horrible word that had sent them off on this trajectory.

"Could she have had a fight with my father?" he asked.

"Maybe. She was crying and sounded too upset to say much, though I can't imagine what she would fight with George about. She's always gotten along with him."

"I know. That surprises me."

"Surprised me too. I know he hated her being engaged to Dirk, but since Austin was born, he's changed. He's crazy about that kid and would do anything for him. I think that made him more accepting of Leanne. Plus the fact that, for some reason, she loves being on the ranch and helping where she can." Tabitha took a sip of tea then sighed. "Are you still going to take that job in California?"

Her question came at him sideways. "I'm flying out tomorrow to meet with a prospective client." Was that why Leanne was upset?

"I understand the job means moving around a lot."

"At first, yes."

Tabitha looked reflective as she twirled a copper-colored strand of hair around her finger.

"You look like you're thinking about what you want to tell me," Reuben said.

"Sometimes I think before I speak." She flashed him a tight smile. "Did Leanne ever tell you what life was like for us? Living with our dad?"

"A bit. She told me it was hard. That there were times you were hungry because there wasn't enough food."

"Yeah. I also remember waking up one time and falling down the stairs because the house we lived in before didn't have stairs. Getting lost on our way to school because Dad was gone and Mom didn't have a car and we had to walk and had forgotten the way. But the hardest part was not feeling like a part of anything. I think that's what my mother struggled with the most." Tabitha was quiet as she released her hair. "Did Leanne tell you that our mom left our dad a couple of times?"

"No. She never did."

"She came back, but each time she did the next move was that much harder on her." Tabitha rested her chin on her hand and held his gaze, her eyes looking past him as if delving into her past. "My mom had a couple of potted roses. She always said that when we reached our forever home, she would plant them. She took them along every place we moved. After she died, Leanne and I didn't water them because we always thought it dumb that she put so much stock in those silly plants." Tabitha blinked and looked down at her tea, giving it a lackadaisical stir with her spoon. "I wish we had taken better care of them. We didn't have much of Mom after she died. Leanne and I often wondered if Mom died because she got uprooted so many times and her love wasn't strong enough to regrow. So I wonder if Leanne doesn't have the same fear. That her love wouldn't be enough to withstand the moving around that your job would entail."

Reuben felt a chill sneak down his spine. He and Leanne had faced so much, and now that they were finally together, he felt as if a huge part of what had been missing in his life had been restored to him. Did Leanne think she might not love him enough?

The thought gutted him.

"She loves the ranch," Reuben said, his voice quiet.

"It's security for her. She loves being rooted and grounded. Loves being a part of the cycle of life on the ranch. Loves her garden and seeing Austin growing up on a place his father grew up. But that's not everything to her." Then, to his surprise, Tabitha reached across the table and took his hands in hers. "I'm not telling you this about Leanne to change your mind about what you want to do or the decisions you need to make. I'm trying to give you some insight about my sister's life and her reasoning."

Reuben nodded, feeling as if his world was shifting. Realigning. The past few days had given him a different point of view. He wasn't sure he liked it, but he knew one thing for sure.

He wasn't letting Leanne go again.

Her head ached and her heart was sore.

Leanne stared out of the windshield of her car, not sure where she was going, but knowing that she had to keep moving. She'd been driving since she called Tabitha, aimlessly driving for the past few hours.

Reuben had sent her a text message when they were supposed to meet for supper. She had been tempted to ignore it but she didn't want him to worry.

So she had sent him a cryptic reply then turned her phone off.

Snow swirled in a cloud behind her car, blinding her to what was behind, and all she could see ahead was illuminated by the twin cones of her headlights, stabbing the gathering dark.

She slowed down as she came to a crossroad. One road led north to Calgary, the other south to the Crowsnest Pass.

Maybe she could find a hotel in Calgary. Stay there for the night. She would call Tabitha when she got there.

She choked down a sob as she made her choice, thinking of what George had told her. Of what had happened between her and Reuben the past few days. The truths that had come out.

With each step in Austin's growth, each change in his life, each stage he went through, she thought of Reuben and what he had chosen to miss. And each time that happened, her resentment and anger with him grew.

For so many years Dirk had been the hero, Reuben the villain and the ranch her home and safety net.

Now Reuben was back and she had discovered that she had been wrong about him and how he felt about Austin. Finding out that Dirk had created the circumstances of their estrangement had been the first tremor.

Discovering that her actions hadn't been any different from those of Reuben's mother, and seeing the condemnation back on George's face after she had worked so hard to gain his respect had shaken her. Then for him to demand she leave…

She felt as if she had lost her foundation.

Help me, Lord, she prayed. *I don't know who I am or where I belong.*

Living at the ranch had given her purpose and she felt as if she had finally found a place for herself and Austin. But no matter how hard she worked or how much she did, her future was always at risk because she had built her life at the ranch, on a shaky foundation.

She had built her house on sand and had not trusted in God. She had put her hope in living on the ranch to "save" her. She had put off telling George the truth about Austin because she thought it would jeopardize her position there.

And then Reuben had come back into her life, and for a while she clung to the hope that she could have both him and the life she had created.

He was leaving tomorrow to take the final steps toward a job that would mean a lot of moving. A job that would take them both away from the ranch.

And what will you choose?

She wanted to have things work for her. And yet she struggled to justify that the life she had built on the ranch would be best for Austin. But could she expect Reuben to live in a home where he'd been treated so poorly from the beginning?

"I love him. I love him and I want to be with him."

She spoke the words aloud in the silence of her car and they seemed to resonate. Fill the space. She waited, and slowly everything else slipped away.

She'd always wanted to be with Reuben. She had fought against it and tried to work around it. She had been selfish by putting her trust in the wrong place.

She needed to go back to Cedar Ridge and back to Reuben.

As soon as she made that decision, it was as if a deep peace suffused her. She had stopped fighting, trying to plan and arrange. Only one thing was necessary. That she and Reuben and Austin be together.

She peered through the dark, trying to find a place to turn off the highway so she could turn around.

Two small lights reflected at her. A dark shape suddenly appearing on the side of the road.

A deer bounded onto the road, racing to avoid her.

Leanne hit the brakes and swerved the car. The back end blew around and the front tires spun in the snow. She fought to regain control and then, a split second later, she slid sideways into the ditch.

It took a few moments to realize what had just happened. She inhaled deeply, her hands tingling in reaction.

Then the reality of her situation soaked in. She was an hour from town, stuck in a ditch and who knows how long from getting a tow.

She grabbed her purse, yanked out her phone and turned it on. Her heart sank as the screen came to life and she could see that she had no cell service and how late it was. Which meant she had no way of calling Reuben or, even more important, a tow truck.

She dropped her head against the headrest, tamping down her fear and frustration. She had to get back to Cedar Ridge before Reuben left for Los Angeles. She simply had to.

Still nothing from Leanne.

Reuben shoved his phone into his pocket and turned his attention back to the breakfast he had ordered, wondering why he'd actually thought he'd be hungry.

Last night he stopped by the hospital after seeing Tabitha, but George was sleeping so he went back to his hotel and dialed Leanne's number. When she didn't answer, he sent a text message but again, nothing.

This morning he called Tabitha to see if she'd heard anything. All Tabitha would say was that Leanne had texted her early this morning saying she was okay. Nothing more.

Which only made him angrier that she hadn't bothered to get in touch with him.

He pushed his food around on his plate, then sent another futile text to Leanne.

In two hours he had to leave for Los Angeles, and once there he had to make the final commitment to the job. Once the contract was signed, there was no turning back.

A Christmas song came on the radio playing in the café. Christmas was two weeks away. Where would he celebrate it and what would it look like? Would he and Leanne and Austin be together?

He swallowed down an unwelcome knot of pain, and as took a sip of his coffee, he sent up yet another prayer for peace and for wisdom. He kept his head down, feeling rude as people walked past him, a few calling out a quick greeting. He looked at his phone, trying to look like he was a man with purpose.

If only he knew what that purpose was.

"Reuben, I thought you were leaving today." Owen Herne dropped into the chair across from him, making it impossible for Reuben to ignore him.

"I don't need to be in Calgary for a couple of hours yet," he said.

"Are you going to see George before you go?"

"Yeah. I'm picking up my…my…nephew to take him there." He caught himself. He had almost said his son.

He wanted so badly to tell someone. Wanted to make that declaration. Except he couldn't. Not until George knew.

"I stopped and saw George yesterday. After the meeting. He was pretty upset," Owen said.

"Did he say why?"

Owen lifted his one hand in a vague gesture. "Something about your mom and Leanne being the same. I didn't know where he was going with that, so I thought I would change the subject. So I asked him what he was getting Austin for Christmas. And then he started crying." Owen shook his head, still looking surprised. "Seriously, I never thought I'd see your old man do that."

"Crying?"

"Yeah. He just looked ahead, tears rolling down his face."

Reuben couldn't wrap his head around the idea and couldn't even begin to imagine his saddle-leather tough father crying.

"They say that people who have had heart

attacks tend to be more emotional," Reuben said, still feeling shocked.

"Nah. This was more than that," Owen said. "It was kind of hard to see. I hope he's okay."

"I'm going there now so I guess I'll find out." He wiped his mouth and signaled to Adana to get him the bill.

"But you're not done with your breakfast."

"What are you, my mother?" Reuben teased.

"Just seems a shame."

"You can have it if you want it."

"Nah. I'm good." Owen got up and Reuben followed suit, still confused about what Owen had just told him.

Something about your mom and Leanne being the same...crying...

What had George been talking about?

But before he left the café, he pulled his phone out of his pocket and quickly dialed Leanne's number.

Once again he was sent directly to voice mail. Stifling a sigh of frustration he shoved the phone back into his pocket, put the truck in gear and went to pick up his son and visit his father.

Three generations of Walshes, he thought as he left Cedar Ridge. Hard to keep that out of his mind.

* * *

Leanne tried not to rush. She didn't want to end up in the ditch again. Fortunately she'd had enough gas in her car to keep it running while she waited for the tow truck to finally show up. The driver, who was the closest and most available, couldn't come for four hours.

She'd had to walk down the road until she came to a slight rise, and there she managed to get one bar of service. Enough to call a tow truck and give him her cell number, for what good that would do. Then she went back to her car, running it a few times, just to stay warm.

When the tow truck finally came, the sun was pinking the clouds on the horizon and her fuel gauge was flirting with Empty. It had taken him only minutes to pull her out of the ditch, which only served to increase her frustration and anger with herself. She'd filled up her tank up as soon as she could and kept on driving, surprised at how far she had driven last night.

As she drove she could still hear George's voice telling her to leave. Hearing the anger and betrayal in his voice. His rejection of her and her son.

She fought down a sob of despair as she finally reached the turn-off to Cedar Ridge.

She glanced at the clock on her dashboard. Would Reuben be at the hospital or at the ranch by the time she got to town? She wished she could call him but her phone was dead.

As she played through the possibilities, she doubted Reuben would return to the ranch. He would be leaving for the airport this afternoon, so he would probably stop in to see his father.

His father?

Leanne shook off the confusion. One thing at a time. And right now that one thing was to get to the hospital. To see Reuben.

She prayed it wouldn't be too little too late.

Chapter Thirteen

George was sitting up in a chair when Reuben came into the hospital room, carrying Austin. The remnants of his father's lunch sat on a tray parked on a table and his father was staring out the window. Reuben couldn't read his expression but as soon as Austin saw George he called out, "Gwampa, Gwampa. Missed you."

George's head swiveled around and the smile on his face when he saw his grandson eased Reuben's worry. He still looked pale, however, and as they came closer, Reuben saw lines of weariness bracketing his father's mouth and eyes.

"Hey, little guy," George said, holding out his hands for his grandson, but Reuben held Austin back from climbing onto George's lap.

"Missed you," Austin said, leaning instead against George's leg.

"So, I understand Leanne came to see you yesterday." Reuben didn't have time to play around. He needed to get directly to what he wanted to talk about.

George's mouth narrowed and anger twisted his father's features. He readied himself to pull Austin back, but then George shook his head as if ridding himself of whatever reaction Reuben's comment made.

"I can't talk about it. Not in front of the boy."

Dread trickled down Reuben's spine. "Did Leanne tell you the truth?" he said, digging in the pocket of his coat for the toy car that Austin had taken from Tabitha's place. He handed it to his son to distract him, and thankfully Austin walked over to the other empty chair in the room and started running his car up and down the arm rest.

"The truth? About him, you mean?" George lifted his chin toward Austin who was making engine noises, engrossed in his play. "Yes. She did." George looked up at him and the dread became a deep-seated fear. "And I told her the truth about you."

"Me? What truth about me?"

"Your mother. She fooled around on me.

I'm not your father any more than Dirk is his." He pointed at Austin, who had his back to them. "Didn't Leanne tell you?"

"Tell me what?" Reuben could only stare at his father, trying to sort out what he was saying. "I haven't talked to her yet."

George closed his eyes and rubbed them with the back of his hand. "The truth is… I'm not your biological father."

Shock. Surprise. Confusion. Reuben didn't know which emotion to deal with first.

"What?"

"Your mother cheated on me. She got pregnant by someone else."

He stared at his father as his entire world crumbled around him. Was God playing some cosmic joke on him?

In the span of a week he'd gained a son and lost a father.

"Who? Who is my father then?" he asked, his voice cracking, still trying to find the ground under him. Again.

George shrugged, then glanced over at Austin who was, so far, oblivious to what they were saying. "Some guy who came through town one day. Your mother said she didn't love him and that he didn't want to have anything to do with her or you. So she stayed with me. But I knew you weren't mine because, well, your mother and I hadn't been intimate for some time. She hated being on the ranch. Hated the ranching life, and it got to the point where she hated me."

Once again Reuben felt like his life had been rocked to its core.

"All these years, why didn't you ever tell me?" Frustration and anger edged his voice as he tried to find his bearings.

"I was too ashamed."

Which made sense to Reuben. His proud father wouldn't want to admit that the boy his wife carried, the boy born while he was married to his mother, wasn't his.

"So why didn't my mother take me with her?"

"She was selfish and she didn't want you from the moment she found out she was pregnant."

Reuben fingered the scar his father gave him, thought of the anger George had rained down on him. Thought of how concerned he was that he would be the same kind of father.

And in that moment he felt a curious untethering from this complicated man who had defined so much of who he was.

He wasn't his father's son after all.

He was his own person. He was a child of God first and foremost. But George Walsh's angry, at times vindictive, blood didn't run through his veins.

Reuben hadn't even realized how much it had haunted him until it was no longer there. As he looked at his father, he suddenly saw him in a different light.

"Is that why you were so hard on me?" Reuben asked. "Because I wasn't your biological son?" He leaned against the wall, looking for some support as he worked his way through this new place.

George looked up at him, his eyes narrowed slightly. "You were a difficult kid. Dirk was always easier. He was a happy, pleasant kid. He listened. Did what he was told. You fought me at every turn. Just like your mother did. But I was on my own with two young boys to raise. It wasn't easy. You weren't easy."

This was hardly justification for how he was treated but, in fairness to George, he had given a boy who wasn't his son a home. And, if Reuben were truly honest, some good memories.

Then George's expression softened. "But you did love the ranch—I'll give you that. More than Dirk ever did."

"Still do," Reuben admitted.

"Why didn't you stay?"

"Because of how you treated me. Because

of how you were always favoring Dirk over me." Though now he understood better why, especially given George's temperament. In fact, if he wanted to be gracious, George could be given some credit for giving a home to a child that was no relation to him.

"I know I did." George sighed as he nodded. Then his eyes fastened on Reuben as if looking for something. "But I was trying. Believe me, I was trying."

Reuben wanted to believe him. "You were so angry with me when I came back last week."

"You made me feel guilty. About how I treated you." He sighed again. "Having Austin around made me realize how much I missed by being so hard on you. And now, after coming so close to death, I've been thinking. I know what I did to you was wrong. You were just a little boy when your mother left. It wasn't your fault, what she did." Silence followed this, broken only by Austin's jabbering in the corner of the hospital room. "I shouldn't have been so hard with you. I should have been more patient."

Reuben couldn't have been more shocked. But even as he processed this, another reality inserted itself.

"And how do you feel about him?" Reuben asked, looking over at Austin, who was still playing with his toy, seemingly oblivious to the emotional storm swirling around him.

George sighed, then looked over at Austin. "It was hard finding out that he wasn't Dirk's son." Reuben heard the confusion in his voice, saw the frustration on his face. "I had always seen him as a little bit of Dirk still with us."

"Do you love him less now that you know the truth?"

George's features altered, as he seemed to process this question. "He's such a sweet, dear boy."

Reuben watched the play of emotions on his father's face and felt a surprising flow of sympathy for George's confusion.

"I don't want you to take him away," George said. Then he looked up at Reuben. "Even though I know what I did, I don't want you to take him away."

"Why not? He's not your biological grandson. At all."

"But I care about him. I always saw him as…as a second chance. To do what I should have done with Dirk and with you. To do the right thing."

Reuben felt a mix of surprise and compassion for the confusion his father was expressing. For the feelings he was baring.

Then George caught his hand, his fingers tight. "You have some good memories don't you?" he asked, an imploring tone in his voice.

Reuben looked down at their entwined hands and as his shirt sleeve slid up he saw the scar on his own wrist. Painful memories intertwined with the ones that George was hoping he had.

"I remember going fishing. You, me and Dirk. We rode the horses up to that little lake up in Jackknife Basin. We had a fish fry and rode home under the stars."

"Yeah. I remember that. And the time we had that roundup when that one kid we hired came along? He had a ukulele and insisted on taking it everywhere."

Reuben laughed. "I forgot about that one. He kept wanting to play while he was riding."

"He wanted to be Roy Rogers," they both said at once.

They fell quiet and then Austin, bored with his play, came back. "Gwampa still sick?" he asked, leaning against George's leg again. "You come home now?"

George smiled, curling his hand around the boy's neck. "Tomorrow. I'm coming home tomorrow."

"Uncle Wooben come home tomorrow?"

Austin asked. "Stay at the ranch with me and mommy?"

Reuben looked down at his son, trying to imagine that scenario.

He suddenly felt less and less certain of the path he had chosen for himself. A path he had hoped to share with Leanne and Austin. The three of them away from Cedar Ridge and all the memories and pain. Starting over.

"You have to leave soon, don't you?" George asked. "Go to California?"

"I do." He folded his arms over his chest, thinking.

"Do you think Leanne will come with you?"

"I hope so."

George looked down at Austin, and Reuben thought of his father's earlier entreaty. Could he do it? Could he stay?

"You know, I was so proud when my dad transferred part of the ranch over to me," George was saying, rubbing Austin's shoulder as he spoke. "I still remember sitting in that lawyer's office signing the final papers. He got up and shook my hand and told me to take care of it. To someday pass it on to my son like his father had passed it on to him. I knew early on it wouldn't be Dirk. He didn't love it like you did. But I didn't know if I could ever pass it on to you."

"Because I wasn't your true son. I wasn't a Walsh."

George nodded. "But I could see you loved the ranch," George continued. "It was in your blood even if it wasn't Walsh blood."

Reuben looked at the man he had always considered his father, and he thought of their past and wondered if they could write a new future.

It was what Leanne wanted.

He kept coming back to that. He thought of what Tabitha had told him about their life moving around with their father and how hard it was on their mother and on them.

Lord, show me what to do, he prayed. But even as he formulated the petition, he knew what he needed to do. What was the best decision for Leanne. For Austin. For George. And, if he was honest, for himself.

"Would there be room for me? On the ranch, if I stayed?" he asked.

Are you sure this is what you want? he asked himself. *You would be working with this man. Can you trust him?*

Reuben thought of the days he and Leanne had spent side by side, herding the cows, working with the horses. It had felt so right in a way that he knew that his job as an engineer, traveling around the world, leaving Leanne and Austin behind each time, never would.

George didn't look up at him right away, and for a heart-stopping moment Reuben thought he had made a drastic mistake by putting himself out there like he had with this complicated man.

"Yes, there would be room. I've wanted to sell the store for some time now. I can use the profits from that to expand the ranch."

"Sell the store?" Reuben was surprised. Walsh's Hardware had been almost as important to his father as the ranch.

George nodded. "I need to slow down, and I think Carmen could be talked into taking it over."

Then his father looked up at him and Reuben saw the sheen of tears in his father's eyes.

"Would you stay? Be a partner on the ranch?" George asked.

"We would have to trust each other," Reuben said, safeguarding his answer. "I'm not your biological son after all."

"I trust you" was all George said. "And to me, you are my son. The only son I have left."

"Then I think this can work. I want to stay and I want us to be a family."

George smiled gently, looking back down at Austin. "I want this too."

Even as they made this agreement, Reuben thought of Leanne, wondering where she was and what she was going through right now.

His heart twisted at the thought of her. But looking at Austin and his father, he knew that he had made the right decision.

Leanne parked her car in the parking lot of the hospital. Weariness clawed at her, but as she got out of her car, she saw Reuben's large truck and relief sluiced through her. Reuben wasn't gone yet.

She hurried over the snow-covered sidewalks, then into the blessed warmth of the hospital. She nodded at the attendant behind the counter and strode down the corridor to George's room, Christmas music following her. She almost faltered as she thought of Christmas and where she, Reuben and Austin might be sharing it.

Doesn't matter, she told herself. *The important thing is that we are all together.*

As she came near George's room, she heard Reuben's deep voice, Austin's sweet one and then George replying.

Then, to her utter surprise, the sound of laughter.

She paused outside the room, wondering what could possibly have gone on since George had sent her out of here with such anger in his voice.

Had he and Reuben made up? Had they found a way to bury their differences?

Would she even be a part of all of this?

She shook off her questions, reminding herself of what she and Reuben had shared and the feelings they'd always had for each other.

She loved him.

And with that resonating through her, she stepped into the room, shoulders squared, head held high. But she stayed in the doorway, still unsure of her reception.

George saw her first and she braced herself for his anger.

Instead, to her surprise, she saw contrition, not anger, in his expression.

"Leanne, I'm so sorry," he said, his voice breaking. "So very sorry."

Reuben spun around as Austin came running toward her. "Mommy, you here," he called out, arms held wide in welcome. She swept him up, holding him close as she tried to understand what George had just said, a complete contrast to the fury he had shown her a less than twenty four hours ago.

Then Reuben was beside her, his arms around her, holding her close.

"I'm so glad you're okay. I was so worried." He stroked her hair back from her face, his eyes holding hers as if to make sure.

She leaned into his arms, relief and love washing over him. "I'm sorry I left. I didn't know what to do. Where to go," she whispered.

"George told me what he said to you."

"Really?"

"Yes. So where did you go? Why didn't you contact me?"

"I was upset. George was furious when I told him the truth about..." She looked at her son who was running his toy car up and down her shoulder. Then she held him close, so thankful the three of them were back together. "He told me to leave and I did. Then I started driving. I felt like I was no different than your mother. I had done the same thing."

"You are nothing like my mother," he said, giving her a gentle shake. "Don't ever think that."

She gave him a watery smile, her emotions definitely shaky.

"You still didn't tell me where you went," he said.

"Nowhere. I just drove, thinking and praying, then a deer jumped in front of me, I hit a ditch and I didn't have cell service. Then my phone died."

"How did you get out?"

"Tow truck," she said, holding his puzzled gaze. "Thankfully I managed to get through to the driver before my phone died." She almost laughed. This wasn't how she envisioned their reunion. Talking about tow trucks and cell phones.

"I'm sorry I didn't get hold of you," she said, slipping her free arm around his waist. "After what George said, I needed time to think. To process what he told me and what I needed to do."

Then to her surprise and joy, Reuben bent over and kissed her.

"I love you," he said.

And in that moment every concern she had about her decision, every second thought was blown away.

"I love you too," she returned, laying her head on his chest. "And I want you to know that I'll go with you wherever you go. I'll live wherever you want to live. As long as we can be together."

"So you would move to Los Angeles with me?"

She nodded without hesitation. "Any place

you want. I know that I love you enough. I know you'll take care of Austin and me. And I want us to be a family, wherever that may happen."

Reuben kissed her again, his arms surrounding her and Austin. "You are amazing," he whispered in her ear.

"We need to be a family," she repeated. "No matter where. No matter what."

Reuben drew back and turned to George, who was leaning forward as if trying to hear what they were talking about.

"What are you saying? What's going on?" he demanded. "Come over here and tell me."

Reuben, his arm still around her shoulders, escorted her to George's side.

"Leanne was telling me that she'll go with me wherever I go. Even if it's California."

Leanne could see the puzzlement on George's face and she thought of what it would do to him to have Austin move away. In spite of his anger with her only yesterday, she felt sorry for him. He would be losing so much.

"She's saying that we need to be a family." Reuben gave her a loving look, his arm firmly around her. "And I agree."

George still looked confused. "But I

thought you were staying here. In Cedar Ridge. At the ranch."

Reuben brushed another kiss over Leanne's head. "We are."

"What are you saying?" Now it was Leanne's turn to be confused. "I thought we were moving. And don't you have to leave soon? For your interview in Los Angeles?"

"I'm not going."

"What? I don't understand."

Reuben looked from her to Austin then to George. "George and I have decided that I'm going to become a partner on the ranch. I'm staying here." He gave her a careful smile. "If that's okay with you. But if you have your heart set on Los Angeles—and given the snow we've been dealing with I wouldn't blame you if you do—we can still go."

All she could do was stare at him as the implications of what he was saying seeped into her sleep-deprived brain. "Stay here? On the ranch?"

"Together."

She didn't know whether to laugh or cry or shout out her thanks so she did all three.

"Happy, Mommy?" Austin asked, concern edging his voice as he grabbed her by the face, still holding his car. The wheel mashed into her cheek, which made her laugh even more.

"I'm happy, buddy," she said, giving him a tight hug.

She set him down and then slipped her arm around Reuben. She couldn't stay close enough to him.

"I can hardly believe this," she said. Then she turned to Reuben. "Are you sure this is what you want?"

He nodded, smiling down at her. "I'm sure. George and I have a few things to iron out but I'm confident we can make it work."

"So long as you learn to listen to me," George grumbled. Austin had come to stand beside him again and was now running his toy car up and down George's arm. Leanne was about to reprimand her son when George took his hand and moved it to the arm of the chair.

"Why don't you play with your car here?" was all he said.

"What happened while I was gone?" Leanne looked from George to Reuben, still puzzled at the obvious equanimity prevailing in the room. A far cry from the anger George had hurled at her yesterday.

"We can catch up later," Reuben told her. "For now, I think we have something more important to discuss. I think our son needs to be brought up to speed before we talk about another thing."

Leanne shot a glance at George, who was teasing Austin by putting his hand in the way of the car.

"You want to do this now?" George asked, his attention still on Austin.

"I don't want to wait any longer." Reuben looked to Leanne as if seeking her approval.

"I don't either," she said.

Reuben walked to the other chair in the room and brought it over, setting it down beside George. "Sit down here," he said to Leanne and, as she did, he picked up Austin, set him down on Leanne's lap and knelt down beside them both.

Leanne sent up a quick prayer for strength, wisdom and the right words and then brushed Austin's hair back from his face, her hand lingering on the lighter patch of hair so like his father's.

"Austin, honey, you know I love you," she said.

He nodded, his attention on his car, looking delightfully unconcerned.

"You know that I'm your mommy, right?"

Another casual nod.

"But you need to know something else. Uncle Reuben isn't your uncle. He's your daddy."

This caught his attention. He laughed. "No. Uncle Wooben."

Reuben took one chubby hand in his and curled his own hand around it. "No, sweetheart. I'm your daddy."

Austin looked puzzled but then nodded. "Okay" was all he said. Then Austin pushed Leanne away and slid off his lap, obviously done with the conversation.

Leanne looked from Reuben to George, puzzled. "Well, that was rather anticlimactic."

"I don't know if he fully realizes what just happened," Reuben said with a light laugh.

"He will. And when he does, it will seem normal to him," George said.

Leanne grabbed Reuben's hand for moral support then turned to George. "Yesterday you were angry with me when I told you the truth about Austin. If you truly want us to live on the ranch with you, I need to know that you are okay with all of this. His being Reuben's son."

George didn't say anything right away and Leanne wondered if she had pushed things too far.

"I am," he said finally, his voice quiet. "I was wrong to yell at you. But it was a shock."

Leanne acknowledged that with a nod. "I believe that."

"But I want us to be a family. You are all I have, and even though Reuben might not be my son through blood, he is my son in every other way. I want you all to stay with me. I can't imagine…" His voice broke. Then he regained his composure. "Anyway, I'm glad you're staying. All of you. Leanne, you've been a real blessing to me, Austin, as well, and I don't want you gone."

Leanne reached over and took George's hand, squeezing it gently. "I'm glad about that." Then she looked over at Reuben who was watching her, love in his eyes, and she felt a peace and joy that she hadn't felt in years.

"I love you," she said to Reuben, still holding her father-in-law's hand.

"I love you too," he returned, bending in for a gentle kiss.

"Okay. That's enough of that, you two," George said, his voice gruff. "We have plans to make."

Epilogue

"I think you must have cleaned out the entire stock of farm animals from your store," Reuben said to his father as Austin ripped open yet another box. The little guy squealed his delight at the sow with four little piglets nestling in the tissue paper. He set them up beside the barn that he and Leanne had painstakingly assembled, joining the herd of cows and the horses, chickens, dogs and cats already lined up.

George just laughed, leaning back in his chair, the lights of the Christmas tree playing over his lined face. "It's my duty as a grandparent," he said. "And it was the last chance to get the discount. Once I sell the store, I won't have that anymore."

Remnants of wrapping paper were strewn under the Christmas tree now empty of gifts.

Christmas music filled the room and a fire snapped in the fireplace, all combining to create a feeling of warmth and home.

Reuben compared it to the Christmas he spent last year in a hotel room watching a forgettable Christmas movie on television. It had been bleak and depressing and lonely. This was light and love and peace. The contrast almost made him cry.

Austin got up and brought a handful of animals over to Reuben. "Play with me, Daddy," he said.

Austin had been calling him that for the past couple of weeks but it still sent a thrill through his soul.

"I don't know, sweetheart," he said. "I think it's getting close to bedtime, and tomorrow we are going to Uncle Cord and Ella's place for Christmas dinner."

His son shook his head in denial and scooted back to the farm he had painstakingly set up.

Leanne came in carrying a tray of mugs. "Hot chocolate for you," she said, handing one to George. "And coffee for you," she said to Reuben.

Then she turned to Austin. "And bedtime for you." She was about to pick him up when George stood up, grunting as he did so.

"I can take care of that," George said.

"That's okay," Leanne protested, holding up her hand as if to stop him.

"You've done enough. Besides I need some one-on-one time with my grandson, and you and Reuben need to talk."

He gave Reuben an exaggerated wink, which made him groan. Nothing like being obvious.

Leanne shot Reuben a puzzled frown but he simply shrugged as if he had no idea what his dad was talking about.

Austin protested, but only slightly, as George helped him pick out an animal to take to bed with him. Then, together, they walked out of the family room.

"Sit here," Reuben said to Leanne.

She did, still looking puzzled. Especially when he got up and went to the Christmas tree and pulled a tiny box out of the branches. Then he sat down beside Leanne.

But he could tell from the way she was pressing her fingers to her lips and her shining eyes that she had some idea what lay inside the box.

He carried on anyhow, determined to do this right. He got down on one knee and opened the box to show her the ring inside.

It caught the lights of the tree and reflected them over her face.

He'd had a speech all prepared but as he looked up at her, her eyes shining and his heart pounding, he decided to stick with simple.

"Leanne Rennie Walsh. I love you so much. I want to spend the rest of my life with you and Austin. Will you marry me?"

"Of course I will" was all she said, her lips quivering. Tears spilled from her eyes, leaving a glistening line down her flushed cheek.

He slipped the ring on her finger, and she held it up, making it catch the lights from the tree. "It's so beautiful," she breathed.

"Not as beautiful as you," he said. He stood up and gathered her in his arms, holding her close, a sense of utter peace and contentment washing over him.

They shared a soft, gentle kiss, then both drew back, looking deep into each other's eyes as if to cement their relationship.

"I love you so much," she said. "I don't know if I'll ever get tired of saying that."

"Me neither." He kissed her again.

She smiled, stroking his face with her hand, growing serious. "This was a long time coming," she said. "But I'm so thankful. So grateful."

"God has definitely worked in mysterious ways to get us here."

She laid her head on his chest, her hand on his heart.

"You know, after we figured out what Dirk had done, I was furious. I couldn't forgive him for what he did, but in the past couple of days I've realized that if Dirk hadn't done what he did, I wonder if we would have ended up here. At the ranch."

Leanne sighed lightly, then drew back smiling up at him. "Maybe that's true, but I'd like to think that we would have found a way to make our life wherever we would have ended up."

"I'd like to think that too, but I'm thankful that out of all of this, George and I have found a way to make peace and forgive each other. To be father and son at last."

Leanne held his gaze and her smile was like a bright beacon of love. "You are an amazing man, Reuben Walsh, and I'm so glad that we found our way back to each other."

"Me too. I'm so thankful and humbled that we've found a place where you and I can raise our own family. I will forever be grateful for that."

"Our family. I like the sound of that. I promise you that I'll always be there for you."

"And I promise that I'll always take care of you," Reuben said. "You and Austin and any other children we might have."

"Other children?" She gave him an impish smile. "How many other children were you planning on our having?"

"Let's take things one kid at time," he said.

She laughed then pulled him close, and as the lights twinkled in the tree behind them and the gentle music holding the promise of Christmas floated around them, their kiss became a seal on those promises and a hope for the future.

Together.

* * * * *

If you loved this story, check out
COURTING THE COWBOY
SECOND CHANCE COWBOY
from bestselling author
Carolyne Aarsen's miniseries
COWBOYS OF CEDAR RIDGE
and these other stories of love on the ranch
from Carolyne Aarsen
WRANGLING THE COWBOY'S HEART
TRUSTING THE COWBOY
THE COWBOY'S CHRISTMAS BABY

Available now from Love Inspired!

Find more great reads at
www.LoveInspired.com

Dear Reader,

This book is about looking for security and seeking forgiveness and healing from the past. Leanne needed to be forgiven for the secret she kept, and Reuben needed to find a way to forgive a father who had hurt him so much in the past. It's also about secrets and the cost they can have on relationships.

I also wanted to show that forgiveness is a journey, and I hope you, as a reader, realize that this journey is really just the beginning for Reuben and his father.

I hope you enjoyed the book. If you want to learn more about me and my writing, visit my website at www.carolyneaarsen.com to find out more about my books.

Blessings to you,

Carolyne Aarsen